Here's what critics are saying about Catherine Bruns

"I highly recommend this series, and best!"
—*Kings River Life Magazine*

"Readers are sure to enjoy this playful tale...this book is bound to please anyone that is looking for an easy, satisfying read on the beach."
—*InD'tale Magazine*

"If you like your cozy mysteries complete with a cast of zany characters this is one for you. And guess what? Recipes are included which makes me really wish I could bake."
—*Night Owl Reviews*

"TASTES LIKE MURDER is an intriguing start to the *Cookies and Chance Mystery* series. I want to visit more with all of the quirky characters just to see what crazy and outrageous things they will do next!"
—*Fresh Fiction*

"Twistier than expected cozy read—great for beach or by the fire"
—*The Kindle Book Review*

BOOKS BY CATHERINE BRUNS

Cookies & Chance Mysteries:
Tastes Like Murder
"A Spot of Murder"
(short story in the Killer Beach Reads collection)
Baked to Death
Burned to a Crisp
Frosted with Revenge
Silenced by Sugar
"Drizzle Before Dying"
(short story in the Pushing Up Daisies collection)
Crumbled to Pieces
Sprinkled in Malice
Ginger Snapped to Death

Cindy York Mysteries:
Killer Transaction
Priced to Kill
For Sale by Killer

Aloha Lagoon Mysteries:
Death of the Big Kahuna
Death of the Kona Man

Ginger Snapped to Death

A Cookies & Chance Mystery

USA TODAY BESTSELLING AUTHOR
CATHERINE BRUNS

Ginger Snapped to Death
Copyright © 2019 by Catherine Bruns
Cover design by Janet Holmes

Published by Gemma Halliday Publishing
All Rights Reserved. Except for use in any review, the reproduction or utilization of this work in whole or in part in any form by any electronic, mechanical, or other means, now known or hereafter invented, including xerography, photocopying and recording, or in any information storage and retrieval system is forbidden without the written permission of the publisher, Gemma Halliday.

This is a work of fiction. Names, characters, places, and incidents are either the product of the author's imagination or are used fictitiously, and any resemblance to actual persons, living or dead, business establishments, or events or locales is entirely coincidental.

Acknowledgements

As always, thank you to retired Troy police captain Terrance Buchanan for answering my never ending questions. Huge kudos to beta readers Constance Atwater and Kathy Kennedy, who always make the book better with their comments.

Karen Clickner-Douttiel provided the delicious recipe for gingerbread cookies and a very special thank you to the talented Kim Davis for use of her scrumptious candy cane brownie recipe.

Last but not least, thank you, readers, for continuing to follow Sally's journey. May your Christmas and every other day of the year always be full of "good fortune."

CHAPTER ONE

Josie beamed as she handed me an oblong gift-wrapped box. "It's just a little something, Sal."

"But I thought we weren't exchanging Christmas gifts this year." Guilt consumed me as I tore off the green paper decorated with miniature Santas and the words *Ho ho ho* coming out of his mouth in a bubble. "Besides, you've already done so much—the baby shower, the gorgeous cake, and the car seat."

Josie's blue eyes softened as she placed the dirty mixing bowl in the three-bowl sink. We were standing in the back room, or kitchen area, of my bakery, Sally's Samples. As head baker, Josie Sullivan's unique talent was the sole reason I still had a business after three and a half years. We'd been best friends since the age of eight, and she'd never once let me down.

"I could say the same thing about you, you know," she said softly, her mouth quivering at the corners. "After all the stuff you've given my boys over the years, I wanted to do this. It really isn't a Christmas present, nor anything for your precious cargo, but I happen to think it's perfect. Careful when you remove the top—it's a bit hazardous."

"What?" Puzzled, I unwrapped the package and lifted the lid to find a six-inch serrated silver cake server. The handle had been engraved in pink lettering with the words *Property of Baker Sally Donovan*.

"Oh, Jos!" I gently lifted the server out of the box and examined it, careful not to cut myself on the sharp and shiny edge. "It's beautiful."

Josie's freckles stood out as a wide grin broke across her face. "You did such a great job helping me with that wedding cake last week that I wanted to get you something special. I'm so proud of you, Sal. You've really come into your own as a cookie specialist, and now you can even bake and decorate cakes too."

"Let's not get carried away. I'll never be as good as you." The fact that Josie had so much confidence in me was mind-boggling.

She leaned across the wooden block table. "The server caught my eye last night when I was at the mall, and they were offering free engraving. You've worked so hard and deserve the recognition. I mean, three and a half years ago, you could barely bake a cookie without burning it. You've come so far."

My cheeks burned at the compliment, and for a moment I couldn't speak. I'd always wanted to run my own business, and without Josie, it wouldn't have been possible. From the beginning, it had been clear to both of us that she would handle most of the baking and all the decorating, while *I* would wait on customers and manage the financial side of the business. "I never would have made it this far without you." My voice shook with emotion. "You've been my inspiration."

Josie followed me into the storefront as I tried to find the perfect place to display the server. It was too pretty to keep in a drawer in the back room, and I wanted the entire world to see it. A two-tiered oak shelf was attached to the wall over the counter, which held my Keurig and espresso machines, cash register, and a supply of plastic bags and pink boxes for customers' goodies. My husband, Mike, had built the shelf for me. Actually, he had built almost everything in the bakery after a fire had destroyed my former one.

There were already some special trinkets on the shelf, which consisted of a framed certificate we'd won on *Cookie Crusades* baking show a couple of years back, and a wooden cookie platter with the words *Sally's Samples makes the best cookies* painted in the center. My sister, Gianna, had given me the platter when my bakery first opened. I tried to reach up and place the server next to the platter, but my bulging belly wouldn't allow it.

"Here, let me, little mama." Josie took the server from my hand and frowned. "Ouch." The blade had brushed against her palm, and she peered down to examine it. "Lucky it didn't break the skin. I forgot how sharp this thing is."

"Did you hurt yourself?" I asked.

She shook her head. "Nah. It's all good. Maybe this really is the best place for it. I don't want Mommy to open one of the drawers in back and slice her finger by mistake."

We went back into the kitchen area. "You know me too well," I said. "I was clumsy before, but these days I'm ten times worse."

"No, you're not. You're pregnant. There's a big difference. No one feels graceful and light-footed when they're expecting."

"I haven't seen my feet for weeks."

She laughed and lifted a tray of gingerbread men she'd finished decorating. The room was filled with the scent of sweet frosting and molasses. A light snow had fallen earlier and coupled nicely with the twinkling lights Josie had run around the front porch of the bakery. It certainly gave the place a Christmassy air. "Isn't today your due date?"

"Yesterday was," I corrected her and rubbed my belly with satisfaction. I'd been waiting for nine months to meet my son or daughter. Mike and I had decided not to find out the baby's sex. It was our first child, and we wanted to be surprised. "It could be anytime now."

"Well, in that case, go home. I'm officially firing you." She filled a piping bag with frosting and started to decorate another tray of gingerbread men.

I burst into laughter. "Oh, really?"

Josie looked ready for action, her auburn hair pulled back into a neat bun behind her head and the pink Sally's Samples ball cap carefully positioned over it. Her matching pink apron was immaculate, like her decorating. She was slim and trim in jeans and a red sweater and ready to conquer the world.

I was quite the opposite in a wrinkled Sally's Samples T-shirt and black maternity pants that had started to feel snug the last couple of weeks. I'd bought them online during my first month of pregnancy, partially because of the company's motto: "No matter what your size, these pants will take you to the very end." Baloney. They were one stretched seam away from a tear and an embarrassing moment.

That didn't bother me though. I could deal with an

oversized body for a few more hours or days if necessary. My pregnancy had been a relatively easy one, despite my 40-pound weight gain. My poor sister Gianna had had terrible morning sickness from day one during hers, but it had been the opposite for me.

Everyone constantly said that I glowed and looked radiant. I'd never been happier in my entire life. Mike told me that I grew more beautiful every day, and I loved him all the more for it. My Grandma Rosa said I was a pure ray of sunshine. But when my darling outspoken father had seen me yesterday in a red and white sweater, he'd jokingly asked if Santa Claus had come early. He had a knack for always saying the wrong thing, but I think he meant it as a compliment. At least I hoped so.

"I feel fine," I protested. "Actually, I've never felt better. Don't they say that you get a sudden burst of energy right before you go into labor?"

Josie snorted back a laugh. "Yeah, right. I was sick as a dog the entire nine months with each kid." Josie had four boys whose ages ranged between three and twelve. "When I hit the eight-month mark, all I wanted was to sleep 24 hours a day. What's you're secret?"

"No idea. I'm excited about the baby. And happy. So happy, Jos."

She smiled warmly. "Well, you deserve to be. You've waited a long time for this to happen, Sal. No one deserves it more."

"Thanks." I picked up a tray of fortune cookies to put in the display case out front.

Josie grabbed the other side of the tray. "Put that down. You're not supposed to be carrying anything."

"Oh, stop being silly. The tray is light."

"Don't argue with me," she said firmly. "Go home. I talked to Mike earlier, and he agrees with me that you should stop working today."

I struggled not to roll my eyes. "Yes, I know. He and I have this discussion every single night. You're both way too overprotective."

"And you're way too stubborn. Let go."

Josie gave a tug on the tray at the same time that I

relinquished my hold. The fortune cookies flew into the air, somersaulted, and fell to the floor with the tray, accompanied by a loud bang.

"Crap," Josie mumbled as she got down on her hands and knees to pick them up. When I started to bend my knees to help, she held up a hand. "Sal, I'll get the rest. You might hurt yourself."

Good grief. Everyone was treating me like an invalid. Yes, I was heavy and moved slow these days, but I felt fine. And I wasn't surprised that Mike had called Josie. He'd pointedly told me this morning before he left the house that he wanted me to stop working today, and I'd refused. We'd almost gotten into a fight, and we never argued.

"Why can't I continue to work if I feel good? What's the big deal?" It didn't make sense to me. My Grandma Rosa had recently regaled me with stories about how my grandfather treated her during her pregnancy with my mother. Grandpa, who had passed away when I was a toddler, hadn't been the type to fuss over a woman or give her any special treatment. He'd been old school, born in Sicily, and it was simply the way his generation behaved. Still, it had appalled me when she'd mentioned how Grandpa had her shoveling snow right alongside him, at nine months pregnant. When she went into labor, he'd dropped her and her suitcase off at the hospital entrance and gone back to work. If she could survive all that, the least I could do was carry a tray of fortune cookies into another room.

The entire batch was ruined, but at least fortune cookies weren't costly to make. They were more time consuming than anything but our customers loved to receive a free one with each purchase. As I picked up a cracked one, I couldn't resist pulling the strip out, and I burst into laughter when I read it. "Did you mix up a couple of words on this one, Jos?"

She shot me a questioning look. "Why, what does it say?"

I read aloud. "'You better watch out—Santa Claus is coming…for you.' Shouldn't it be 'to town' instead?"

Josie shrugged as she dumped the rest of the cookies into the trash. "I ordered a bag of messages from the novelty shop. We've been so busy lately with the holiday rush that I didn't have time to make my own this week. Sorry. I should have asked you first."

"Don't be silly. You know that's not necessary." Even though we worked side by side, I never knew how she managed to get so much done on a daily basis. The thought made my head spin.

Josie pointed at the door that led to the alley. "Okay, getting back to what I said. You're fired. Go home. Or better yet, go to your parents' house, mooch dinner from your grandmother, and then go home and cuddle with your man. Call me when you go into labor. Are you having any contractions?"

"No. Some lower back pain and my ankles are swollen, but that's about it."

"Well, I don't expect to see you tomorrow. Let me rephrase that. I will *not* be seeing you tomorrow."

"It's not that simple," I argued. "This is my business. I just can't abandon it for an entire month. I'll bring the baby in with me."

She rolled her eyes. "We're not having that discussion again. You have no idea how tired you're going to be when that baby gets here, which is why you should rest up now."

Josie knew what she was talking about, but I refused to admit that I couldn't handle a baby *and* the bakery. I did intend to enjoy my child and bring him or her to work with me. There was an empty apartment upstairs that I planned to use for that purpose. As much as I trusted Josie with the business, I couldn't stay away for that long. The bakery was also my baby. I'd find a way to make it all work.

I grabbed my coat and my purse. "Okay, stop badgering me. I'm leaving. Happy? And yes, you will see me tomorrow, at least for part of the day."

Josie blew out an exasperated sigh. "Sal, you are the most stubborn—"

I blew her a kiss. "Love you. Have a great night." With a laugh, I shut the door behind me and slowly made my way over to my car, thankful for my flat but ugly rubber-soled boots. I'd stopped caring about making a fashion statement when I'd been in my fourth month. As I settled myself behind the wheel—not an easy task these days—I thought about how lucky I was to have such caring people in my life.

    Mike had texted while I'd been talking to Josie. My husband owned a one-man construction company that kept him busy almost every day of the year. He was currently finishing up a couple of jobs and then not taking on anything new until after Christmas next week. He wanted to be at home with me and the baby for a few days. The thought of the three of us sharing Christmas together always brought tears to my eyes. It was a dream that was finally coming true.

    I dried my eyes with a tissue and then placed the car in drive, slowly proceeding down the alley. It was only five o'clock, but the sky had already darkened. My hometown of Colwestern, located in western New York, was always festive looking at this time of year. Christmas lights sparkled from every direction. Josie had decorated the small fir trees in front of the bakery with colorful lights, and the bagel shop across the street had their giant, plastic Santa Claus on the front porch, like every year. The sub shop down the block had an enormous silver star that flashed on and off from the top of their building. I loved seeing these familiar treasures every year. Christmas had always given me a special feeling, but this year it was more than usual.

    We'd had snow earlier today. It had only been a couple of inches, but enough to turn the area into a winter postcard scene. I turned on the radio and smiled when I heard my favorite Christmas song playing, "Rockin' Around the Christmas Tree." Although my singing voice was horrible, I sang at the top of my lungs as I drove down a side street with Peacock's Dry Cleaners to my right. Life couldn't be any more perfect right now.

    The traffic light changed to yellow as I approached. I probably could have made it but decided not to tempt fate. The dry cleaners closed at four, and the building was dark except for one dim light inside. There were no Christmas lights or decorations of any kind, and I shook my head in disgust. The entire building appeared forlorn and lonely. Lawrence Peacock was about my grandmother's age, and everyone knew that he would never retire. He'd owned the business for as long as I could remember and grumbled every year that Christmas did nothing but make the electric company richer.

    The inside of the car was stuffy, so I rolled my window

down partway for some air. As I waited for the light to change, the baby kicked. I smiled and sighed, reaching a hand down to my belly. I would never get tired of feeling that little person move inside me.

"Hey there. You *are* going to come out before Christmas, right? Your daddy and I can't wait to meet you."

"Get out of the car!"

Puzzled, I looked up to see a man standing next to my car door. A gun was pointed at my head, and the man at the other end of it was none other than Santa Claus.

My entire body froze with shock as I stared into a pair of listless dark eyes that eerily resembled the night. I tried to speak, but words stuck in my throat.

"Are you freaking deaf, lady? I said to get out of the car!"

Okay, he didn't actually say *freaking*—it was a word ten times worse. But that was the least of my worries. My hands, stuck to the steering wheel at the ten and two o'clock positions, had started to shake. A shot rang out, and I screamed. The bullet had gone through my front passenger window, which shattered on impact. Another Santa was standing directly in front of my vehicle. *Holy Christmas.* I was being carjacked by the big red man himself.

"What the heck are you doing?" I shrieked.

"Get out of the car, lady," the first Santa said again, "or I'm going to blow your freaking head off."

"Okay, okay." Somehow I managed to place the vehicle in park. The light had turned green, but there was no one behind me. It was just my luck. My phone was in my purse only inches away, but if I tried to go for it, he might shoot me. I had to think of my baby first.

Slowly I raised my hands in the air. "Please don't hurt me. I'm pregnant."

"Get. Out. Of. The. Car." He enunciated each word slowly, as if speaking to a child. "We ain't gonna hurt you or the kid as long as you cooperate."

Having no choice, I slowly opened the door. Santa Number One was clearly lacking patience as he reached in and grabbed me by the hair. I screamed in pain and struggled, but the gun pressed against my head forced me into immobility. "Let me have my purse, please."

Santa Number Two got behind the wheel while the first one put a choke hold around my neck. "Forget it, lady. Seems like you ran out of luck."

His voice was young, and he talked like a street kid. I wondered if they might be part of a gang. although I'd never heard of any in Colwestern. "Please! Let me have the purse. You can keep the money."

The gun was resting mere inches from my head. Santa Number One's face was olive skinned underneath the fake beard, and he smelled of peppermints. How appropriate. I also noticed that his beard was a cream color, not the usual snow white, making me think it was a second-hand suit. He glanced over at my purse and spotted my phone sitting on top. "Right, so you can call the cops? Forget it, fatso," said Santa Number One.

He gave me a shove, and I lost my balance and fell into the snow. I groaned and spit the fine white powder out of my mouth as the engine of my car came to life. Tires squealed and smoked as the two Santas and my Kia roared out of sight.

"I'm *not* fat. I'm pregnant!" I screamed into the frigid night air, but there was no one to hear me. I was lying on my back in the snow, struggling from side to side to raise myself. I felt like Randy in the movie *A Christmas Story*. "I can't get up! Somebody help me! I can't get up!"

A man came running from the direction of the dry cleaners. "Are you all right, miss?" He bent over me in the snow and extended his hand as I mutely stared up at him. He was about my father's age—mid to late sixties, with a head full of shocking snow-white hair and matching whiskers that surrounded his mouth.

I let out a small whimper. Oh God. What was with all the Santa look-alikes today?

"Please help me," I cried. "Someone stole my car. I'm nine months pregnant, and I can't get up."

"Okay, ma'am. You stay calm, and I'll get you out of this mess in a jiffy." He reached down and pulled on both of my arms. He must have been part superhero, because within seconds I was back on my feet. A bit wobbly and shaken, but at least I was standing.

"Thank you." My breath came out in short painful gasps, and I wondered if I was having a panic attack. It hadn't totally registered for me what had happened. Despite my heavy down coat and gloves, I was freezing and afraid I might be going into shock. Petrified, I ran my hands over my belly. The baby gave a sharp kick in response, as if to assure me that he or she was fine. Relief spread through my body. "Thank you so much, Mr....uh…"

"The name is Nick, ma'am." He massaged his white whiskers thoughtfully. "What happened?"

"I got carjacked by a couple of guys dressed like Santa Claus."

His bright blue eyes went wide with horror. "Oh, my goodness. I hate it when people paint the old fellow in such a poor light. You should probably go to the hospital to get checked out. I took the liberty of calling 9-1-1 when I heard the shot, but should I take you to the hospital myself?"

A flash of bright lights and a siren from behind forced me to turn around. A police car stopped at the curb, where my own car had been parked minutes ago. To my relief it was not your average police car. "I know this officer," I said to Nick over my shoulder. As I started to take a couple of steps toward the cruiser, I realized how badly my entire body was shaking. The driver's door opened, and the officer rushed over to me. Oh yes, I knew this police officer very well.

Brian Jenkins was more than just another Colwestern police officer. He was a good and trusted friend who had come to my aid many times in the past. I'd first met him over three years ago when I'd come back to Colwestern after divorcing my miserable, cheating ex-husband. Brian had investigated a homicide on my bakery's porch and quickly made it known that he was interested in more than the bakery's chocolate chip cookies. Although he was handsome and a great guy, he'd never had a chance when Mike and I rekindled our relationship from high school.

Brian put a hand on my shoulder. "Sally, what are you doing here? Where's the man who called the incident in? Where's your car?"

Too many questions to answer in my current frame of mind. Tears welled in my eyes. "I got carjacked by a couple of Santa Clauses."

His green eyes shimmered with astonishment and reflected off the lights on the top of his squad car. "Oh my God. No offense, but you're a regular magnet for disaster." He glanced down at my stomach. "You and the baby are both okay?"

"I think so. Can you take me to the hospital? And I need to call Mike. My purse and phone were in the car."

He muttered a four-letter expletive under his breath. "What a couple of scumbags, assaulting a pregnant woman. Of course I'll take you." He gently placed a hand under my elbow and escorted me toward the passenger side of his vehicle. "Easy now. Careful you don't slip."

"Oh! I almost forgot. I need to thank Nick for his help."

Brian looked at me with a confused expression. "Nick who?"

"He's right over there." I turned around and pointed to where Nick has been standing next to the fire hydrant. But Nick was nowhere in sight. I stared at the snow where he'd found me and saw only my footprints. The street in front of me started to spin. This made no sense. "Where did he go?"

Brian laid a hand on my arm. "Sally, you probably just imagined him. Sometimes people suffer hallucinations after a traumatic event."

"*No*. He was here." The blood started to roar in my ears. I hadn't imagined him. In desperation, I scanned the area again. As I turned around, dizziness overwhelmed me, and my vision grew fuzzy. Brian was wrong. I'd held a conversation with the man. He hadn't just disappeared into thin air. The baby kicked as I breathed in the cold air and tried to fight off the feeling of claustrophobia that suddenly assailed me. Was I in labor or hallucinating like Brian said?

"Sally?" Brian gave my arm a little shake. "Stay with me, okay? You're looking a bit green. Are you going to pass out?"

"No," I mumbled as the darkness closed in around me. "I just need…air." I reached out to Brian, and his strong arms caught me before I could hit the pavement.

CHAPTER TWO

───

"Princess, this doesn't make sense," Mike said. "Santa Claus stole your car and then he helped you out of a snowbank?"

I struggled to get comfortable in the hospital bed, but it was no use. The belt around my stomach monitoring the baby was extremely uncomfortable. "I know it sounds crazy, but yes. The guy who saved me looked like Santa Claus, and his name was Nick."

Mike was visibly tired. Lines of worry creased his handsome, rugged face, and his curly black hair was disheveled from running his hand through it so many times. He'd arrived at the hospital in a panic, even though I'd assured him on the phone that the baby and I were both fine. I'd had no contractions, but since I was past due, the hospital had prepared me for a delivery room in case. The baby had kicked a few times in Brian's squad car, but the fetal heart monitor had indicated everything was normal. The ultrasound had shown no issues either. Part of me wished to have the baby now so that I could be home with my little family in time for us to enjoy Christmas. But he or she clearly wasn't ready to make an appearance yet.

Mike placed a hand gently on my stomach, his fingers brushing against the belt. "You're sure you're not in labor?"

"I don't think so. Everything seems to be okay." My voice quavered slightly. "What am I going to do? Those jerks took my car!"

Mike's midnight blue eyes blazed into my mine, and he pursed his lips together. "I don't give a damn about the car. I'm just grateful that you and the baby are okay. When I find those sons of—"

The blue curtain was pushed aside, and the nurse, whose

name tag said *Hannah*, peered in at us. "How are we doing here?" she asked cheerfully and examined the monitoring machine next to my bed, pressed a few buttons, and then checked the readout without comment. "Mrs. Donovan, you have some visitors in the waiting room. Would you like them to wait until you're settled into a room upstairs?"

"Visitors?"

She nodded. "Several. The waiting room is full."

Mike rubbed a hand over his eyes wearily, and I stifled a groan. I had been scheduled tonight to have a last-minute fitting of my matron-of-honor dress for Gianna's wedding. I'd texted her from Brian's phone on the way over and told her what had happened, assuring her I was fine. We were cutting it close since she was getting married on Christmas Eve, but I couldn't help that my body kept expanding every day. Gianna must have told the rest of our family what had happened. I appreciated the concern, but only wanted to go home.

"They can come in," I told Hannah, "but I don't want to stay here tonight. The nurse who was in earlier said everything looked fine. Can't I go home?"

"Well…" She hesitated and gave me a small smile. "Let's see what the doctor says first, okay? It's his call, not mine. Now, I'll send some of your visitors back. Two at a time is the maximum, plus your husband."

I leaned back against the pillow as Mike stroked my hair. "Can I get you anything, princess? Something to drink?"

"No, I'm—" Before I could even finish the sentence, the curtain moved and Gianna rushed in, followed by Grandma Rosa.

"Sal!" Gianna whispered, her long chestnut-colored hair brushing against the side of my face as she hugged me around the neck. "Thank God you and the baby are okay. We were so worried."

Grandma Rosa shook her head in dismay. "It is a sad world when a pregnant woman is mugged by Santa Claus."

Boy, was that the truth. It also gave new meaning to having the Christmas spirit.

Gianna smoothed the hair back from my forehead. "Are you in any pain?"

I shrugged. "My hand is a little sore from the fall, but otherwise I feel fine. I wish they'd let me go home. And I'm sorry about the fitting."

Her enormous chocolate brown eyes widened in amazement. "Sal, who cares about that? I'm just glad you're okay. Besides," her voice was barely above a whisper, "the so-called wedding is turning into a three-ring circus."

Gianna and her fiancé, Johnny Gavelli, had been excited about the idea of a Christmas wedding. As bride attendants, Libby—a college friend of Gianna's—Josie, and myself were all going to wear red silk dresses. The church was to be decorated with poinsettias, colorful Christmas wreaths, and alternating red and white bows on the pews. Gianna's son, Alex, was only nine months old, but had a little black tuxedo for the occasion and was to serve as ring bearer. Okay, he couldn't walk yet, but that was the general idea.

Our mother, Maria Muccio, had been a "momzilla" of the bride during the planning of my wedding to Mike, but she seemed to have learned her lesson this time. She'd backed off from harassing Gianna. The honor of "zilla" now belonged to Nicoletta Gavelli, Johnny's grandmother. Nicoletta had lived next door to my parents for over thirty years. She and I had had a love-hate relationship ever since she'd found Johnny and me playing doctor in her garage when I was only six years old. Of course, I had no idea what was going on at the time, but she'd instantly branded me a hussy and kept that mindset for the next 25 years.

Nicoletta had a love-hate relationship with most people, so her attitude toward me wasn't unusual. My grandmother was the only person who was never afraid to set her straight. But this time even Grandma Rosa was having trouble getting Nicoletta to behave. She seemed to think that the Gavelli/Muccio wedding was the red-carpet event of the year and should also be something straight out of *The Godfather*. All Italian food would be served—no exceptions—and topped off with a rum-filled wedding cake for dessert. There would only be Italian music played, and none of that shameful sinner garbage that deranged young people liked to listen to.

Gianna had humored her in the beginning, but lately

they'd had some terrible arguments. Nicoletta was old fashioned and didn't even believe that the baby should be present since he'd been born before the wedding. We'd suspected that she'd be difficult, but Nicoletta had taken the cake, so to speak. My sister was one step away from jumping off a cliff.

"It will be fine," Grandma Rosa assured her. "I will talk to Nicoletta again."

Gianna gritted her teeth in annoyance. "Please don't even say her name, Grandma. It's like scraping fingernails on a chalkboard." She reached over to touch my belly. "And my nephew—or niece—is fine? Can they give you something to induce you?"

The idea of being induced didn't hold much appeal. "I'm not sure I want to go through that if I don't have to." Of course I was dying to meet my baby, but the process sounded extremely painful. I'd heard some unpleasant tales about inducing from my bakery customers, many of whom were always eager to share their horror stories of pregnancy.

"Your mother and father are waiting to come in," Grandma Rosa announced. "Gianna and I will leave so that they can see you. Try not to worry, *cara mia*. Cars can be replaced. You and the baby cannot."

She gave me a peck on the cheek, and Mike kissed her as well. When they pulled back the curtain to leave, Dr. Chandler was standing on the other side. He had delivered both Gianna and me and, to my delight, had no intentions of retiring yet. His amber-colored eyes smiled encouragingly at me under a thick head of white hair. Dr. Chandler stepped aside for Gianna and Grandma Rosa to exit. Gianna looked back at me and mouthed, *Let me know what he says.*

"So, how's our patient—whoops. I mean, how are our *patients*—feeling?"

"Restless," Mike said, as he kissed my hand.

I sat up straight in the bed and smiled wide. "And both want to go home."

"Hmm." He checked the printout in front of him, perhaps the same one Hannah had removed from the machine earlier, and then looked at my chart. "There's no indication that you're in labor, even though it is your due date. The baby might not come for another week or two. Then again, you could get home and contractions might start immediately."

"We only live five minutes away from here," Mike said helpfully.

Dr. Chandler scratched his head. "Well, we can give it a try. Be sure to call me right away if you experience any pain or if something seems off. When's your next checkup scheduled for?"

"Friday."

"Oh yes, that's right," he mused, still looking down at the chart. "If everything still looks good with the baby then, we'll probably let you go a few more days before inducing. But if contractions begin before the appointment, call the hospital immediately. Remember, we're always here." He gave a low chuckle, his obvious attempt at a joke.

Mike looked at me wide-eyed. "Inducing doesn't sound like much fun."

"They strip the membranes," I said. "It forces your water to break."

He looked at me in horror. I should have spared him the graphic details. I wished my customers hadn't shared that tidbit with me either.

Dr. Chandler gave me an encouraging pat on the shoulder. "Let's not worry about that yet, okay? Make sure you take it easy. And avoid all stress." He looked at me questioningly. "You're not still working at the bakery, are you?"

Mike's mouth formed a thin, hard line. "She was fired today."

"Hold on," I objected. "I promise not to overdo, but I do have a business to run."

"Josie is perfectly capable of handling everything," Mike said, "along with that new woman you hired."

His comment made me wince. Dodie Albert was an elderly woman who had started work at my bakery last week and should never be mentioned in the same breath as Josie. In short, Dodie was a walking disaster. She was an excellent baker and decorator, and always tried hard to please, but she was ten times clumsier than me at nine months pregnant.

On her first day, she'd knocked a container with five pounds of flour onto the floor when the phone rang, claiming it had startled her. Then there was the tray of eggs that somehow slipped out of her hands. While brewing coffee for a customer, she'd forgotten to place a cup under the Keurig lever, and the liquid had spilled all over the floor. To make matters worse, Josie had then walked in from the back room with a tray of cookies for the display case. The cookies and Josie had both hit the floor in record time.

Except for Mickey, our driver, we'd never had good luck at hiring people. Mickey was a freckle-faced college kid who'd also been our most reliable employee. Over the years we'd succeeded in hiring deranged killers and even one person who'd been an unfortunate victim. Mickey was a brave soul to want to work for us. It looked like my maternity leave might be shorter lived than I'd planned.

"What if I only went in for an hour or two each day?" I pleaded to both the doctor and my husband. "That would be okay, right?"

Dr. Chandler glanced from me to Mike, sensing that a war might break out soon. "It all depends on how you're feeling," he said wisely. "If you're in any pain, then no. But if you feel fine, I don't believe an hour or two would be a problem. Try to sit down while working, if possible, and don't overdo it. Okay, be careful on the drive home, and I'll see you soon." He winked at me, shook hands with Mike, and then left the room.

Mike brought my hand to his lips. "Princess, why are you fighting me on this? Why don't you sit home for a few days with your feet up and watch soap operas until the baby gets here?"

"Because it's our busiest time of year," I protested. "We need to pull in as much money as we can."

He sighed and ran a hand over the unshaven stubble on his chin. "Yeah, I get that, but I happen to care more about you and the baby than the money."

The curtain rustled, and we glanced over to see Brian peeking in. He grinned sheepishly at both of us. "Sorry to interrupt. Can I come in for a second?"

"Sure," I said.

Mike rose from the chair and extended his hand to Brian. There'd been a time when he would have preferred to punch

Brian in the jaw instead of shaking hands. He'd been jealous when Brian had tried to court me after my return to Colwestern. Even after Mike and I had gotten back together and professed our former high school love for each other, he was still wary of Brian for a while. The two would never be good friends, but at least they respected each other. With Brian's wedding coming up next month, it appeared that his torch for me had finally been extinguished.

Mike's voice shook slightly. "Thank you for coming to Sal's aid. I can't stand to think of her lying in the snow with no one to help her."

"But there was someone," I insisted. "I told you that Nick was there. He helped me out of the snow. I couldn't get up by myself. Then he disappeared."

Mike glanced from me to Brian and then back at me again. "Sal, are you sure you didn't hit your head on something?"

"Oh, for crying out loud," I said in annoyance. "Why doesn't anyone believe me? I know what I saw. Brian, I was standing when you found me, right? How would I have gotten up without any help?"

Brian had to think about this for a minute. "She's right, Mike. It would have been difficult because of her size—er, condition." His face turned a shade of crimson.

Mike sat back down and reached for my hand again. "Okay, princess. Whatever you say."

"Don't patronize me," I snapped, then shut my eyes and blew out a deep breath. "I'm sorry. I didn't to mean to snap at you."

Brian cleared his throat. "Uh, Sally, we found your car."

Finally, some good news. "That's wonderful! Is there any damage to it?"

"Forget the car. What about those losers who assaulted my wife?" Mike asked angrily.

"Unfortunately, there's been no sign of them," Brian said regretfully. "There was a break-in at the Jewelry Palace shortly after Sally's carjacking. The alarm was activated, and two Santa Clauses were caught on camera driving away in your car, Sally. They abandoned it on Jay Road, about a mile away. The good news is that your purse was still inside." He handed me my phone. "The purse is being held for evidence, but I did manage to get your cell. There was no activity or fingerprints found, and I knew you'd want it, so…"

What a relief. Brian had gone the extra mile for me. I hadn't expected to see my purse or the contents again, so that was a bonus. "Thank you so much."

"There was no money in your wallet," Brian said. "Did you have any on you at the time?"

"Only about twenty dollars." It was a small price to pay after everything that had happened.

Mike's nostrils flared. "Did they have another car stashed somewhere? How did they get away?"

Brian shrugged. "It's my guess that one of them might live nearby, or they had someone else helping them. By the way, if it's the same two Santas who held up a gas station the other night, this isn't their first felony. There was also a delicatessen in Colgate that was hit a few days ago."

"Why haven't you been able to catch these guys?" Mike asked in disbelief. "You said you saw them on camera."

A muscle ticked in Brian's jaw. "We did, but when a person is wearing a Santa suit, it's a little difficult to identify their faces. We're calling them the Jolly-less Santas."

"I have a few other choice names for them," Mike remarked.

The baby kicked, and I ran a hand over my belly. "You didn't answer my question. Was there any damage to my car?"

"The right front fender has a large dent in it," Brian replied, "and of course, the side window will need to be replaced, but other than that, it seems to be okay. We'll go over the vehicle for any clues or fingerprints, but you should be able to pick it up tomorrow. I'll give you a call when it's ready."

"Are you trying to say that this was just a random act? That my wife was in the wrong place at the wrong time?" Mike asked.

Sadly, that happened far too often to me.

Brian turned his head in my direction, and I guessed he might be thinking the same thing, though he was too polite to say it. "Yes, it sounds like it was bad luck on her part. We found a rusted-out Chevy parked in the dry cleaner's lot. Mr. Peacock said it wasn't there when he closed tonight. We think the Santas dumped it there for some reason and then decided to wait for their next victim—which turned out to be Sally."

"So, these two sick, twisted pieces of crap carjack a woman, hold a gun to her head, and then shove her into the snow, not giving a damn that she's about ready to give birth. What kind of animals are we dealing with here?" Mike asked angrily.

"Dangerous ones," Brian replied, his solemn gaze resting on mine. "Hopefully we find them before they do something even worse."

CHAPTER THREE

———

    Although I was glad to be home in my own bed that night, I didn't sleep well. My lower back ached, and the baby kicked constantly. Plus, I couldn't stop thinking about those few minutes of sheer terror when I hadn't known if we'd live or die. I'd had a gun held to my head before—too many times to count actually—but this had been different. Before, it had only been me. I hadn't been carrying a precious, innocent life inside me, a baby that I wanted more than anything in this world. The thought that my child might have been taken away was too awful to comprehend.
    Mike and I had been married for about two and a half years, but I'd wanted a baby long before that. It had always been my dream to be a mother. After Mike and I had broken up at our senior prom, I'd immediately gone on the rebound with fellow classmate Colin Brown. We'd dated for five years and then stayed married for another five before I'd caught him cheating on me. Colin had told me from the beginning that he didn't want kids, but I'd been confident that he'd change his mind. I had been wrong, but that didn't matter anymore. Soon I would have everything that I'd always longed for.
    Mike was in the shower, so I went into the kitchen to make him coffee and fix a half caff for myself. I stared idly out the window over the sink into our small fenced-in backyard. Spike, our 14-year-old shih tzu, was outside doing his morning business. It was below freezing, so he didn't waste any time hurrying back in through the doggie door. A light snow was falling, and the small deck out back that Mike had added last summer was already covered with a dusting of white flakes. Having lived in the Buffalo region for most of my life, I was

used to the weather, but I still disliked driving in slippery conditions. Today wouldn't be a problem. I had promised to take it easy, and there was no car at my disposal anyway.

I desperately wanted a real cup of coffee but was limiting myself to two half caffs a day. The thought of decaffeinated coffee had never made any sense to me. Why even bother to drink it?

As I stirred a healthy dose of creamer into my coffee, Mike wrapped his strong arms around me from behind. He kissed me on the neck, and I giggled, then turned around to let his mouth settle over mine. He looked incredibly sexy in a dark blue flannel shirt, jeans, and steel toe work boots. He placed a hand on my stomach and smiled when the baby moved. "You didn't sleep at all, did you?"

"Some," I lied.

Mike ran a finger down the side of my cheek. "Are you sure you're okay? Do you want me to stay home?"

"No. You have a deadline for that job. When you finish, you're stuck at home with me and the baby. At least for a week or so."

His blue eyes turned tender with emotion. "There's nothing I want more, Sal." He kissed me again and then grabbed the travel mug of coffee on the counter. "Call me as soon as you hear from Brian, and I'll take you down to the station to get your car and purse."

With a sigh, I rested my head against his broad chest for a few seconds. Mike smelled wonderful—of that spicy scented cologne I adored. It was marvelous to have a quiet moment with his strong arms around me. He always made me feel so safe and loved, and I especially needed that today. My mind traveled back to last night, but I didn't want to worry him, so I forced a smile to my lips. "Gianna said she'd take me over, so there's nothing for you to worry about."

To my surprise, his eyes clouded over. "Of course I'm going to worry. When I think about what could have happened to you and our baby last night—" His voice choked up, and he held me tightly against him, his head resting on top of mine.

A tear rolled down my cheek before I could stop it. "It's all over, sweetheart. We're both fine. Nothing is going to happen to either one of us." A niggle of doubt crept into my mind, and for some strange reason, I remembered the fortune cookie from yesterday. *Santa Claus is coming.* What were the chances—*No.* I wasn't going to start that again. It was purely a coincidence. The fortune cookies could *not* predict the future.

Mike kissed me again. "I'll check in with you a little later. Promise you'll call me right away if you start having contractions."

"I will. Love you."

"Love you too, princess. Now put your feet up and relax today."

After he'd left, I wandered into the baby's room. It was my new favorite place in our house. The room radiated with love and filled me with a sense of peace. With a broad smile, I ran my hands over the rail of the handsome oak crib Mike had made for our baby, along with the matching dresser and changing table. Despite all the jobs he constantly had lined up at his construction business, he'd found several hours to create these beautiful pieces for our child. A true labor of love. I hadn't asked Mike to do it. He had simply told me that he wanted to.

A huge lump settled in my throat, and I desperately tried to shake off the doom and gloom feeling. The baby would be here soon, and I needed to take control of my life and be thankful instead of worried.

I went into the bathroom to take a shower and then dressed in stretchy maternity jeans and a patterned black and white blouse. I studied myself critically in the mirror and cringed inwardly when I thought about the fitting for Gianna's wedding. My sister had no idea how I was dreading her special day. I was thrilled that she was marrying Johnny, who worshipped the ground she walked on. It didn't seem right to be so self-conscious about my size, but my dress was now officially the size of a tent.

I was in the process of finishing my second English muffin, and fully engrossed in *The Price is Right*, when my phone buzzed. Brian's name popped up, and I pressed Accept Call. "Hey, what's up?"

"Your car is ready to go," Brian said. "I had it brought back to the station for you. And your insurance company already had a glass company out to fix the window, so feel free to pick it up whenever you want."

"Thanks. That was really nice of you."

"It's not a big deal. I'm glad you and the baby are all right, Sally." He paused. "I was really worried when you passed out last night."

An awkward silence fell between us. No, I must be imagining things. Brian was finally over me. After all, he and Ally Tetrault were getting married soon. Ally was a nurse at Colwestern Hospital, and she'd also been a former schoolmate of mine. Earlier this year, Brian had confessed that he was still in love with me and had contemplated leaving town because of it. I was glad he'd decided to stay and only wished that he and Ally had already made it official.

"Let me call Gianna. She's scheduled off work today and said she'd bring me down."

"Okay. See you soon."

I pressed the button for my sister's number and was met with the sound of a screaming baby when she answered. "Alex is teething," she shouted into the phone after I'd voiced my request. "But I'll be right over. Johnny's here, so he'll stay with him." Johnny was a history teacher and had taken a job teaching college classes at night while Gianna worked as a public defender during the day.

"Are you sure? I can call—"

Another high-pitched wail sounded in response, and I cringed. My nephew had a great set of lungs on him.

"No, it's fine. I need to get out of here. I'll be over in about 15 minutes." The phone clattered as if she'd dropped it, and after another scream, she disconnected.

Yikes. Up until now I'd been convinced that I could handle teething, breastfeeding, and anything else my little darling might throw at me. I'd read every Dr. Spock book that was out there. So why did I feel my confidence dwindling after hearing what Gianna was going through?

My phone buzzed again, and my parents' landline number popped up. "Hello?"

"Hi, sweetheart." My mother gave a low giggle on the other end. "How are you feeling today?"

"My back's a little sore, but other than that, fine," I lied.

She cleared her throat. "Good. Why don't you and Mike come for dinner tonight? Grandma is making lasagna. And cheesecake."

Her last word sealed the deal for me. As far as I was concerned, nothing tasted better than my grandmother's ricotta cheesecake. "Okay, I'll check with him, but I'm sure it will be fine."

"Wonderful." She sounded pleased with herself. "It will give Daddy a chance to talk to you about his new idea."

Uh-oh. This didn't sound promising. Unfortunately, my father was full of ideas these days. Domenic Muccio had recently written a book based on his successful blog. The blog was about death, of all things. Dad was obsessed with it in all shapes and forms. Ever since he'd retired from his railroad job, he'd grown a bit weirder each year. My father had gone from keeping a coffin in the living room to driving a hearse to referring to himself as Father Death. Still, every wacky scheme seemed to make him a little more money, and for the life of me, I couldn't figure out how. Maybe I should start taking notes.

"Okay," I said carefully. "What kind of idea this time?"

She giggled again. "Nope. He wants to tell you himself. We'll fill everyone in tonight. I swear, the man is a genius. Come over about six thirty. Now you rest up and don't overdo it. If the baby decides to come before dinner, tell him or her that it's perfectly fine. We'll understand."

Good grief. I rolled my eyes at the ceiling. "Sure. I'll pass the information along."

I was ready in my full-length down coat and fur-lined boots when Gianna drove up five minutes later. It was difficult to get shoes on these days since I couldn't see my feet, but I'd managed.

As soon as I locked the door and stepped foot onto the porch, she came rushing from the car. She took me by the arm and led me down the steps. "Easy, Sal. I've got you."

"Gi, I can walk by myself," I protested.

Her large eyes regarded me solemnly as she guided me into the passenger seat. "I know, but it's icy out, and after everything that happened, you need to be careful."

Okay, this baby needed to come soon. I was starting to

suffocate from everyone treating me like an invalid. I pulled the seat belt across my stomach, but it jerked back. I tried again. No luck. Gianna got into her seat and helped me. "It must have reached its maximum length." I sighed.

Gianna backed the car out of my driveway. "Look, we're all worried about you, Sal. I mean, I've never heard of a nine-month pregnant woman getting carjacked before. It could only happen to you."

Boy, was that the truth. I changed the subject. "What are you doing home today?"

"The baby has to go for shots later this afternoon, and Johnny hates taking him to the doctor by himself, so I took the day off." She rubbed her eyes when we stopped for a red light. She was pale and looked tired. Gianna had gained over 60 pounds when she'd had Alex, but in the nine months that followed, she'd lost it all and then some. My sister attributed most of it to breastfeeding, but I knew the truth. She never had a free moment to herself these days between her job and caring for the baby. I'd never had doubts before, but watching her struggle made me wonder how I would handle everything.

As if reading my mind, she glanced sideways at me and cleared her throat. "Have you figured out how you're still going to work full time and take care of the baby after maternity leave?"

"I'm only planning to take a month off. Then I'll bring the baby to work with me. He or she can sleep in the apartment upstairs."

"Sal," Gianna protested. "Be realistic. They're both full-time jobs. Keep Dodie on part time and hire a babysitter. Johnny said he'd take the baby one day a week if you want."

"I appreciate him offering, but this is *my* baby, and I want to be the one to take care of it."

Gianna smiled sympathetically. "I understand, but trust me, you're going to change your mind in a hurry when he or she gets here. There's no harm in letting someone help you. I hate to admit it, but Johnny's better at the whole parenting thing than me." She hesitated. "Can I tell you something in confidence?"

"You know that you can."

She blew out a breath and made a left-hand turn. "Don't

get me wrong. I love Alex more than anything, but I don't want to be home with him all day every day. Does that make me a bad mother?"

"Of course not," I assured her. "Everyone is different. I'd love to stay home with my baby all day every day. It would be wonderful if Mike could be with the baby too, like Johnny is with Alex, but that's not an option for us." I sighed. "You'd think I'd have planned this better. I've had nine months to figure it all out."

Gianna pulled the car into an empty space on the side of the police station's gray brick building. "No worries. You'll straighten everything out, love."

As I struggled out of the vehicle, I noticed my car sitting a few parking spaces away. The sight of it made me smile. Gianna was waiting at the front door, holding it open for me. We were about to ask at the front counter for Brian, when he came out of a nearby office and spotted us.

"Hi, Sally. Hi, Gianna."

I turned to my sister. "You don't have to stay. I'll be fine."

She ignored my request and drummed her fingernails loudly on the counter as Brian presented me with my car keys. Gianna leaned over my shoulder as I signed a form stating I'd received my vehicle.

"Every inch of that car was gone over, right? And nothing was found that pertained to the Santas?" Gianna asked.

"An evidence technician went over the vehicle," Brian explained. "Remember, these thugs were wearing gloves and hats. Nothing conclusive was found." His mouth twitched at the corners. "You're such a lawyer, Gianna."

She narrowed her eyes at him. "Yes, I am. It's my job, and my sister could have been killed last night. I tend to take these things a bit seriously."

Brian clenched his jaw. "And you think I *don't* take Sally's safety seriously?"

Gianna folded her arms over her chest. "I never said that. Actually, perhaps you're a tad more involved in her life than you need to be."

Heat flooded my cheeks. "Gianna!"

Brian's Greek godlike face had turned the color of a flame and must have mirrored my own. His voice was calm as he addressed me. "Your car is parked on the side of the building, Sally. Now if you'll both excuse me, I have work to do." He turned on his heel and quickly disappeared into the office he'd come out of.

Exasperated, I looked at my sister. "What's the matter with you? It's not Brian's fault that I got attacked."

"No," Gianna agreed. "But it is his fault that he still looks at you like a lovesick puppy. You're happily married and having a baby. He'd better get over this obsession now."

This was all I needed. "Okay, thanks for bringing me down, but I'll be fine on my own."

We exited the building, but Gianna stuck to me like glue until I reached my car. Maybe she was afraid I'd be attacked again. It wasn't likely, especially in a police station lot, but with my track record, I couldn't blame her.

I looked at the fender damage and then made my way around to the driver's side. "It could have been worse. Look, I'll call you later about the fitting. And Gi, please don't embarrass me in front of Brian like that again. If you'll recall, he's been very helpful in the past when I've been involved in some sticky situations. I don't want to lose his friendship."

Gianna pursed her lips together. "I'm sorry, Sal. That wasn't my intention. But I have to wonder if he's deliberately delaying his marriage to Ally because he's still in love with you."

"All right, I am *done* talking about this." I gave her a hug and got into the driver's seat. "Are you and Johnny going to Mom and Dad's for dinner tonight?"

She nodded. "Johnny will bring Alex, and I'll meet them there. After the baby gets his shots, I'm scheduled to meet with a client at five and not sure how long it might take. Please go home and not to the bakery. Promise me."

"Gi, I'm not five years old. If I want to go to the bakery, I'll go to the bakery." I shut the door in defiance before she could say anything more, then waved to her from my seat.

Resigned, Gianna shook her head and slowly walked back to her car.

I knew my sister meant well, but enough was enough. I

had no plans to go to the bakery, but my stubborn streak had kept me from saying so. With a sigh, I stole a glimpse at myself in the rearview mirror. My large dark eyes stared back at me from a rounder, more mature face than before the pregnancy, and I liked what I saw. My skin had never looked better. As my grandmother said to me the other day, "Happiness is an inside job, *cara mia*, and you have plastered it." Of course, she meant *mastered*, but my grandmother often mixed up well-known sayings.

I brushed my hair back from my face and, in the process, caught my earring. It fell onto my shoulder, then the seat before I could catch it. Shoot. I moved as much as I could but didn't see it. Maybe the earring had fallen down the back of the seat. *Great.* Mike had given me the set as a present for my birthday last year. I stretched my hand down inside the space between the bottom of the seat and the cushion.

Instead of an earring, I came up with a white index card. Mystified, it took me several seconds to comprehend what I was staring at. There was a crude drawing of a gun and, underneath it, three lines of hard-to-read printing—almost like a child had written it. The first line had been done with a black Magic Marker, while the lower two lines were in red pen.

2915 Stetson Avenue, Apt. 10
Ho, ho, ho.
Time for you to go.

CHAPTER FOUR

Dumbstruck, I stared at the index card for several seconds, unsure what to do next. This must have been left behind by my carjackers—aka the Jolly-less Santas. A chill swept over me. Were they planning to kill the person who lived at this address? Or was it just a sick prank?

Adrenaline pumped through my veins as I struggled to get out of the car again. The baby gave a sharp kick, and I felt the beginnings of a Braxton Hicks contraction. My abdomen tightened, and I clung to the car door for several seconds while waiting for it to pass. Gianna had already left, so I was on my own. After drawing several deep breaths, I managed to shoot off a quick text to Brian. *Please meet me at my car. Urgent.*

Less than a minute later, the side door to the building opened, and Brian emerged. When he spotted me bent over, standing there with my hand gripping the door, he rushed to my side. His face was pinched tight with worry. "Sally, are you all right? Did you fall?"

"No." My hand shook as I held out the index card to him. "I found this between the seat back and the cushion. It must have been left behind by the carjackers."

Brian's eyebrows shot up as he read the note. "Maybe it fell out of one of their pockets. I can't believe the guys going over the car missed this."

That was the least of my worries. "What do you think it means? Are the Santas planning to kill whoever lives at this address?" Or maybe they had already.

Brian drew his car keys out of his pocket. "Go home. I'll grab Adam, and we'll drive over to this address to investigate. Don't even think about coming along."

His remark stung like a wasp. "Why would I want to come along? I'd never intentionally put my baby in a dangerous situation."

"Sally, I didn't mean to imply—"

Irritated, I waved him off with my hand. "Never mind. Let me know what you find out." Fuming, I got into my car. After taking a few moments to adjust myself and my coat, which was hanging out the door, I reopened the door, then slammed it shut for good measure.

Brian started to say something to me through the glass, thought better of it, and then ran over to his squad car. A minute later Adam Greensburg, his partner, rushed out the door and jumped into the passenger side. Siren flashing, they zoomed off.

I blew out a breath. Okay, I was probably overreacting. Brian hadn't meant to be insulting, but he did know my track record. I seemed to have a knack for getting into dangerous situations, and was more than happy to let him handle this mess. Time for me and my baby to go back home. I was hungry anyway.

I turned the key in the ignition. It clicked, but the motor didn't start. I tried again. Nothing. With a groan, I thunked my head against the steering wheel. I didn't know much about cars but guessed that the battery might be dead. Great. *Why me?*

Quickly, I took stock. Who could give me a jump start? The bakery was closer than Mike's current job. I could phone my father to come get me, but I wasn't in the mood to hear about this morning's death blog post. Gianna had already left, and I hated to bother her again. I pressed the button for Josie's cell, and she answered immediately.

"Are you in labor?" she asked excitedly.

Jeez, they were all acting like I was a bomb about to go off. "No. I was wondering how busy it was at the shop. I think my car battery is dead, and it needs a jump. Any chance you could steal away for about 20 minutes?"

"Of course. Dodie's waiting on customers—well, when she's not dropping their orders—and Mickey's here. He's got a delivery in an hour, so I could sneak out until then. Where are you?"

"I'm at the police station."

"Okay. Sit tight, partner. I'm on my way." She clicked off.

For the next few minutes, I busied myself reading about everyone's dirty laundry on Facebook. The temperature hovered around forty degrees outside, and I was starting to get cold. I didn't want to go back inside the station but might have to if Josie didn't arrive soon. My phone buzzed with an incoming call. *Brian.*

"Sally, where are you?"

"I'm still at the police station. My car won't start."

"Stay there," Brian ordered. "We're bringing this guy in for questioning. You may be able to identify him."

"Brian, if he was one of my carjackers, he was wearing a Santa suit. As you told Mike last night, it would be a little difficult to recognize him."

"It's worth a shot. He denies having anything to do with the incident, but when I suggested he come down to the station, he was only too happy to oblige."

That sounded strange and like a waste of time for me. Plus, I was growing hungrier by the minute. "If he's that willing, then it can't be him. It doesn't make sense. Did you tell him his life might be in danger?"

There was an angry pause on the other end. "Sally," Brian finally hissed out. "Would you please let *me* do *my* job for once?"

Yikes. "Okay, fine. I'll wait here." Someone had a short temper today. Gianna's earlier accusation probably hadn't helped either. And how did she know about Ally and Brian delaying their wedding, anyway? Why was I always the last person to know everything?

Josie's minivan pulled up next to my car. She got out and held a hand up to me. "Stay put, and I'll help you. It's icy."

"For God's sake," I grumbled. "I wish everyone would stop treating me like I'm an invalid. I'm pregnant, not dying."

"Now, now," Josie cooed as she grabbed me by the arm. "The end is near."

It sounded like a great line for my father's blog. "There's been a change of plans. I have to stay here and wait for Brian. I found an address stuffed down in my seat, and we think the person who lives there might have something to do with my carjacking. Brian's bringing him in shortly."

We went inside the station and sat down on the wooden bench against the wall. My back immediately began to ache against the hard surface. As I shifted in my seat, the baby kicked. Josie happened to look over at that moment and grinned when she saw my belly vibrate.

"That little dude or dudette wants to come out. For the record, I can't believe you still don't know what you're having."

"We want it to be a surprise."

Josie snorted. "Oh, babies are full of surprises, let me tell you. And it's more practical to know what you're having. What are you going to do with those thirty onesies and sleepers that you got in all green and yellow? Do you really want your kid to be wearing those for the next year?"

Before I could reply, the front door of the station opened, and Brian's blond head appeared in the doorway. He held the door ajar as Adam led another man, about my age, into the building. When the man's gaze met mine, my stomach twisted into a knot. Dark eyes stared keenly back at me, and when recognition set in, his mouth turned up at the corners.

He was very attractive, with smooth-looking skin the color of a mocha latte the result of his partial Spanish descent. Dark hair that was longer than mine had been pulled back from his face in a sleek ponytail. He was dressed in a faded jean jacket and Levi's with holes in the knees. The white Nike sneakers he wore were untied and looked brand new.

Josie let out a gasp. "Holy crap. It's Damian Ruger."

Damian turned his attention from me to my best friend. "Hey, hot mama, how's it going?" Then he smiled in my direction. "And little Sally Muccio. Not so little anymore, eh? Been baking some serious buns in that bakery of yours, I see."

Anger flickered inside of me like a flame. "Nice to see you too. *Not*."

An officer at the desk motioned to Adam, but Brian remained in place. He folded his arms across his chest as he stared from Damian to me. "You guys know each other?"

"You could say that," Damian smirked. "I'm the first dude Sally ever kissed."

Ugh. After all these years, he still remembered me telling him that. Heat crept up my neck. "We were kids, Damian."

Josie gritted her teeth in anger. "You piece of dog crap. She was only fourteen at the time and thought you were boyfriend material. Hey, we all make mistakes, right? She didn't realize that you were going to turn into a crackhead with the morals of a goat."

Embarrassed, I tugged at Josie's arm. "Uh, these details aren't important. Brian, is it okay if I leave now?" I desperately wanted out of here.

Damian gave a low, husky laugh. "Oh, but they *are* important. Still hot for me after all these years, ain't ya? I heard that you had to settle for Donovan. Sorry that there's only one of me to go around, but maybe you could try cloning me."

Was this guy for real? "It was 16 years ago, Damian. I hate to burst your bubble, but I'm pretty sure I've been over you since, uh—the tenth grade?"

Brian placed his hands in a stop sign formation. "Okay, let's take a break here. Ruger, I'd like to ask you some questions down the hall." He signaled to Adam, who crooked his finger at Damian. Damian winked at me and then followed Adam into what I knew was the interrogation room. Fortunately, I'd never been in there—yet.

"What a piece of garbage," Josie spat out. "I heard that he's been into drugs since high school and that he even beat one of his ex-girlfriends up. I'd bet money that he's the one who carjacked you."

Once upon a time, Damian Ruger had been one of the most popular guys in our high school—and one of the best looking. Mike wasn't at my high school during freshman year, and I'd had a mad crush on Damian. There was something about those bad-boy types that had always appealed to me.

When Damian asked me to the winter formal, I was on cloud nine. We'd started going out after that and had done the typical hand-entwined-in-hand bit in the hallway or necking by my locker. When I'd invited him for dinner, my family had not been so impressed. The next day, my father announced he was missing money from his bedroom, and I'd gallantly defended

Damian's honor. Our dating status lasted an entire two weeks. Shortly after the family dinner, I'd caught him in the cafeteria making out with Magnolia Nunez for all to see. Later that day, Josie had phoned and told me how he'd announced to the entire school bus that he'd dumped me for Magnolia. I'd never been so humiliated in my short teenaged life.

Up until a few years ago, it seemed that it might be my destiny to have men cheating on me. Three years after my brief infatuation over Damian, I'd caught Mike with Backseat Brenda on prom night, but I'd jumped to the wrong conclusion and never given him a chance to explain. Mike had been drinking, but nothing had happened between them. The real icing on the cookie had been my sham of a marriage to Colin, who'd probably been sleeping around on me since our wedding.

Brian placed a hand on my arm. "You can go. I'll call you when I find out what's going on with this guy. He may have been one of the Santas who carjacked you."

"All right." I hoped Damian wasn't one of my carjackers, but if the rumors about him were true, it was possible. But why would the other Santa have a note with his address on it?

Josie put an arm around my shoulders. "Come on, hon. Let's go. I told Rob about your car. He and his brother will be by with jumper cables in a little while and then bring the car back to your house. Do you want me to stay for a while? Dodie will be all right—well, uh, maybe."

"You shouldn't have bothered Rob. Mike would have taken care of it."

"Hey, what are friends and husbands for?"

As we left the station and walked toward her van, I spotted a familiar-looking man talking on his phone and leaning against a black Mercedes. He raised a hand in greeting to me, and I squinted for a better look at him. At that moment, a large white-paneled van stopped between us. After the van moved on, the man got inside his car. I turned to Josie for affirmation. "Did that look like Jerry Maroon to you?"

"Who? The news guy?" Josie glanced toward the car, but the windows were tinted, and it was impossible to see him. Not that it mattered. Jerry Maroon was one man I preferred to avoid. A former anchorman on Buffalo's Channel 11 news, the guy was nothing but trouble. Earlier this year, when Mike had been injured in a robbery, Jerry had tried to sabotage a live interview we'd taken part in to locate the party responsible.

Josie adjusted her sunglasses against the bright sunlight. "I thought he was fired from Channel 11 for harassing one of the female assistants."

"Yes, he was. Last I heard he's working for the *Colwestern Journal.*"

She snorted and stopped for a red light. "Wow. There's a fall from grace for you. Most staff reporters make peanuts. As an anchorman, he probably made twice as much."

I tried to reposition the seat belt across my bulging belly. "He's not a reporter. Jerry has his own daily gossip column. He calls it 'Just the Facts,' but everyone knows that's a load of bull. And I'm guessing that he makes more than the average reporter. Either way you slice it, he's still a creep."

"Lowlife," Josie muttered. "Look what he tried to pull on you and Mike. God knows what he's doing to everyone else."

"Exactly. Gianna had a fit when a client found innocent of embezzlement charges had her name turn up in his column last month. Jerry claimed that she was working as a prostitute to make ends meet. Seems that he had some personal vendetta against her—they went out a few times, and then she dumped him. Anyhow, Gianna was furious and wanted her client to press charges, but she decided to drop the matter. Jerry's nothing but bad news. Yes, pun intended."

"I hope he ends up losing this job over slander," Josie said. "But I've also heard that the *Journal*'s circulation has skyrocketed the past few months, so who the heck knows? Dirty politicians and now dirty reporters. Go figure."

My phone buzzed with another text from Mike—the third one within the hour. *Where are you? Is everything okay?*

Good grief. "Everyone's acting like I'm a bomb about to go off," I said to Josie as I shot off a quick text to my husband. "This baby needs to come soon."

A sly smile formed at the corners of Josie's mouth as she pulled into my driveway. "Aw, they're just excited, hon. Personally, I think it's cute. My family sure as hell didn't act like that when I was pregnant with Danny."

My heart ached for her and all she'd been through. Josie's first pregnancy had been unplanned at the young age of nineteen and resulted in a shotgun wedding for her and Rob. It hadn't been easy for them the first few years, and they'd almost separated once. Danny had recently turned twelve and was the eldest of their four beautiful boys. I'd always envied Josie her family, and now I was finally going to have one too. The thought warmed me from head to toe with excitement.

Josie started to open her door, but I held up a hand. "I'm perfectly capable of making it into the house by myself. If you want a complete rundown, I'm going to eat and then take a nap. If I don't see Rob, please thank him and his brother for bringing the car back."

She laughed. "Okay, point well taken. Call me later, hon." Josie waited until I was inside the front door before she sped off.

After I'd hung up my coat and fed Spike, I spent the next hour feeding my face. I had a generous portion of Grandma Rosa's homemade ravioli, leftover from dinner the other night, and a piece of tiramisu. I was guzzling down a glass of chocolate milk when my phone buzzed. Brian. "Hey, what's up?"

"Sally, I just got done talking to Damian."

"Did you arrest him?" I wanted to know.

Brian sounded confused. "On what grounds?"

"Gee, beats me." The words dripped like acid from my tongue. "Maybe for holding a gun to a pregnant woman's head? Stealing her vehicle? Or perhaps engineering the entire carjacking scheme? He must have had something to do with it."

"Sally, if you can't ID the guy from last night, then no, I have no grounds to arrest him. We found his address on an index card in your seat. That's all. Damian said that you wrote the note."

My eyebrows drew together in confusion. "Why would I do that?"

Brian was silent for a few seconds. "Sally, I have work to do. We can talk about this later."

"No! Why did Damian say that?"

He paused. "Damian said that you're still crazy about him. He seems to think he's some major chick magnet. Once a girl kisses him, they can never get him out of their head."

Oh. My. God. "He's insane!" I blurted out. "That was 16 years ago. Those drugs he does have really affected his brain. Can't you arrest him for illegal usage or something else?"

Brian sighed. "I know what he said is ridiculous, Sally, but he does have a solid alibi for last night. In fact, he was meeting with his parole officer at the same time your carjacking occurred. He's been in and out of jail for the last two years on various assault and drug charges. He insists that he's been clean for a few months, and his parole officer attests to it. The guy has some major issues, but he wasn't one of the Santas who took your car. And if he knows who did, he's not telling."

Steam poured out of my ears. "What an arrogant punk. Not only does he think he's God's gift to women, but he's flat out lying! He must be in on it with the Santas. You have to do something. They could have killed me and my baby!"

His voice was gentle, as if talking to a child. "We're doing our best, Sally. You know that I've always got your back." There was an awkward silence before he continued. "Try to relax, okay? I've got to run. Don't worry. I'll keep you posted."

"But Brian—"

He hung up before I could say another word.

* * *

"I thought Brian was your friend," my mother protested. "It doesn't sound like he fully understands what you've been through, darling."

We were all seated around my parents' cherrywood dining table—my father at the head, with my mother located to his right, and Mike and myself next to her. Across from us sat Gianna, Johnny, and an empty highchair. Grandma Rosa had taken Alex upstairs to change his diaper.

"It's insane," Mike grunted as he helped himself to another piece of lasagna. "Sal and the baby could have been killed. Damian's address is found in her car, and you know she didn't put it there. That guy has to be involved somehow."

"I always knew there was something odd about that boy," my mother mused as she opened her compact and adjusted her false eyelashes. At the age of 54, Maria Muccio looked better than I did most days. Her hair was a tad lighter than my own ebony shade and fell to her shoulders in rich, perfect waves, while mine was curlier with more frizz. Her large dark eyes were set in a heart-shaped face, and she had a perfect size four figure any woman her age—or mine—would kill for. When Mom, Gianna, and I were out shopping a couple of months back, the saleswoman had asked if we were sisters. Mom had giggled and even had the nerve to tell her she was the youngest. To my chagrin, the woman had believed her.

My father snorted and scratched his balding head. "Degenerate punk. I never did get my twenty bucks back from that thieving kid, either."

Grandma Rosa came back into the room at that moment, holding Alex in her arms. Johnny jumped up from his chair to take the baby from her and strapped him into the highchair while Gianna sipped at a glass of wine through half-slitted eyes. She looked like she was in her own private heaven. Gianna had stopped nursing Alex last week and had missed indulging in her Chianti as much as I currently missed my daily doses of caffeine. *Almost.*

"I know it's not what you want to hear, Sal," she said. "But there's nothing else Brian can do. They have no proof Damian was involved in your carjacking."

Grandma Rosa put a finger to the side of her short white hair and moved it in a circular motion. "The boy did seem like a crack job to me."

That got a laugh out of me. "It's *whack job*, Grandma."

"Rosa's right," Mike said grimly. "I'm sure he's done plenty of it."

Grandma Rosa shrugged in response to my correction. "Whatever." The house phone rang from the kitchen, and she disappeared to answer it.

With renewed relish, I dug into my second piece of cheesecake. "I have to try to put this behind me. The baby will be here any day—or minute—and he or she will be a great distraction. Plus, there's your wedding in a few days, Gi."

To my surprise, Gianna frowned at the words and hastily poured herself another glass of wine. Johnny shot me a pained look. What the heck was going on here? Had Nicoletta already succeeded in ruining the entire day for them? This should be a happy occasion, but Gianna acted like she was attending her funeral instead.

Grandma Rosa came back into the dining room and pointed at me. "*Cara mia*, Brian is on the phone for you. He said that he tried your cell, but you did not answer." Her eyes regarded me solemnly. "The officer said it is important."

I threw my napkin on the table with a sigh and slowly got to my feet. What kind of lies was Damian telling about me now? Maybe Brian was calling to say they'd found some way to tie him to the carjacking. I fumed as I walked into the kitchen, rubbing my lower back. The idea that I was still carrying a torch for Damian after 16 years was ridiculous. Only an idiot would believe that.

I grabbed the receiver and sat down in one of the kitchen chairs. Standing for more than a few minutes had become difficult.

"Sally?" Brian's voice sounded urgent. "Are you there? I can hear someone breathing."

"Sorry, Brian. Yes, I'm here. What's up?"

He cleared his throat. "I'm glad that I found you. I took a chance that you might be at your parents for dinner."

"Yes, the entire family is here. What's wrong? Is it related to the carjacking?"

"Yes. Stay at your parents for a little while, please. I'm coming over to talk to you."

I clutched the phone tightly in my hand. "Brian, you're scaring me. What happened? Did you find the carjackers?"

"Sally, I'll tell you everything as soon as I get there."

My patience level was at an all-time low these days. "No! Tell me now. Did you see Damian again? He confessed to the carjacking, didn't he?" Anger coursed through my veins. I couldn't believe that someone I'd once cared about had put me and my unborn child in such grave danger. "I hope that you're planning to arrest him."

"No, I'm not going to arrest him."

I became incensed with rage and could no longer hold back my thoughts. "What? This is crazy! He's a criminal and deserves to get what's coming to him. Why can't you arrest him?"

There was a pause before Brian spoke again. "Because he's dead, Sally."

CHAPTER FIVE

———

"I told you that punk was a bad lot," my father grunted as he dug into his second piece of cheesecake. "He always ran with a bad crowd. I'm sorry he's dead but can't say it comes as a surprise."

Mike sandwiched my hand between both of his. "Are you all right, baby? Maybe we should go home."

I shook my head, still trying to absorb what Brian had told me. "No, Brian's coming over here. He asked me to stay put."

My husband's midnight blue eyes were intense as they stared into mine. "Why? Damian is dead. This doesn't involve you anymore."

I finished off the mug of hot chocolate Grandma Rosa had brought me and merely shrugged. Mike was right. What else was there left to tell me? Damian was dead. Had someone shot him? Was it one of the Jolly-less Santas? Maybe he'd died of a drug overdose. That must be it. So why was Brian coming to see me? My chest constricted, and I sensed that, whatever the reason, it couldn't be good.

My father waved his hand in the air, as if swatting a fly. "Never mind, baby girl. He probably found something to link the guy to your carjacking. Now, forget about him for a moment. There's more important matters to discuss, like my new job."

Gianna frowned at him. "Dad, this isn't a good time for another one of your harebrained schemes. Can't you tell that Sal's in shock?"

My mother ran over to my side of the table on her tiny silver stiletto heels and patted my belly. "Are you in labor, honey? Maybe we should go to the hospital?"

I gritted my teeth and silently counted to ten. I loved my family dearly, but they were slowly suffocating me to death. All I wanted was to go home and forget about the past 24 hours, but the urgency in Brian's voice told me that there was yet another bombshell waiting to fall on my head.

"Nonsense," my father protested. "She needs to know now before my students arrive Saturday at the bakery."

My head shot up. "Did you say students?"

He grinned. "Yep. The local college is letting me teach a course on blogging. I was hoping to use your upstairs apartment."

I glanced across the table at my sister. Gianna's glass slipped, and wine spilled freely on the white lace tablecloth. Distracted, she blotted furiously at the spot with her napkin. "Sorry, Grandma. I'll wash it for you." She pointed a finger at my father. "You are no teacher. You don't even have a college degree, so how are you qualified to teach a course?"

My father grinned and proudly stuck his chest out. His blue T-shirt, stretched tightly over his middle, read in white block letters, *Sally's Samples. Eat a Cookie, Get a Free Fortune*. My father was all about the freebies these days and had asked me for seven—one for every day of the week.

"It's a nonaccredited class," he explained. "They're willing to let me teach and are even going to pay me. The problem is that they don't have any available classrooms on the weekends." His dark eyes searched mine hopefully. "The desks are being delivered tomorrow."

My father never ceased to amaze me. He always had something up his sleeve. "Dad, I'm sorry, but the baby is going to sleep there while I work during the day. You'll have to find another building."

"Princess," Mike said sharply. "That's too much. You already have Dodie working in the bakery. Josie will be fine with her. You should cut back on your hours and only work two or three days a week."

"But it's *my* business," I said simply. "I have to be there. I can do both."

Mike sighed. "It's a lot to take on, especially for a new mother. You're going to be exhausted. How will you handle it all?"

Gianna narrowed her eyes at him. "*I* have a baby and work full time. Does that make me an unfit mother?"

Oh boy. *Careful, Mike.* Gianna was like a rubber band these days, ready to snap at any second.

"Of course not," Mike assured her. "I just don't want her to be worn out, that's all."

Gianna poured herself another glass of wine as the baby squealed and shook his rattle in her face. She kissed his hand and then downed half the drink. "Sure, Sal's going to be worn out," she snarled. "That's part of being a mother. Men don't understand."

Dad raised an eyebrow at her. "My beautiful girl, you're drinking way too much. Stop acting like such a lush."

Gianna slammed the glass down on the table. "Maybe I have a reason to drink. Maybe I've had it with people interfering in my life."

Johnny put a hand on her shoulder and grinned sheepishly at us. "The wedding's stressing her out big time."

Gianna's eyes shot daggers in his direction. "Or maybe it's your Satan-like grandmother who won't give us a moment to breathe?"

"Yep, that's an accurate description." My father clinked his glass with Gianna's.

As if on cue, the kitchen door slammed. "Where my baby?" a shrill female voice called out, and we all cringed. Gianna laid her head down on her arms and groaned. Johnny rubbed his eyes wearily and went to the doorway to greet his grandmother.

Nicoletta Gavelli was under five feet tall, but a pure fireball. She was dressed in her usual black housedress, covered by a wool coat of the same color, black stockings, and Birkenstocks. It didn't matter if it was ten degrees outside or ninety—she always wore the same type of outfit. Her coarse gray hair was pulled back from her lined, leathery face in a tight bun. Dark eyes regarded us all sharply as she shook a bony finger at her grandson. "You come here for dinner and not tell me?" She accepted the coffee mug my grandmother placed in front of her and helped herself from the carafe on the table.

"Fool," Grandma Rosa grunted at her friend. "Are Gianna and Johnny not allowed to eat dinner without you bothering them for once? And I thought that you had a date with Ronald tonight."

Ronald Feathers was Nicoletta's eighty-something-year-old boyfriend. "He have poker game with his buddies," she announced. "He tell me I can come if I serve everyone drinks. What, I a waitress now?"

Mike lowered his head, but I could see the smile forming at the corners of his mouth.

I raised my eyes pleadingly at my grandmother, and she nodded in understanding. I didn't want Nicoletta here when Brian arrived, and Grandma Rosa knew this. She started in the direction of the living room, where the staircase was located, and beckoned Nicoletta to follow her. "Come. I show you quilt I make for Sally's baby."

Nicoletta's eyes shone like a cat's as they regarded me. "You have cravings?" she asked.

I laughed and placed my hands on my belly. "Only for Grandma's cheesecake." But I'd had that when I wasn't pregnant.

Nicoletta nodded approval. "Good. You must give into cravings. If not, baby be born with ugly spots on his head."

My grandmother shook her head in disbelief. "Bah. That is an old Italian wives' tale. Only *pazza* old ladies believe that. Stop scaring Sally."

"Stop calling me old lady," Nicoletta huffed as she followed my grandmother into the living room.

"Thank God," Gianna breathed. "That woman is driving me nuts."

Johnny's face reddened in discomfort, and he stared down at the table. He was caught between two strong-willed women and knew better than to say anything. There was no winning for him.

"Forget about that old broad, sweetheart," my father said to Gianna and then turned back to me. "Sal, the class will only be once a week—on Saturdays. Your mother said she'd be glad to watch the baby if you need her to."

My mother made a face. "Well, honey, of course I want to watch my grandchild, but I thought I'd be assisting you in class."

He winked at her. "Hot stuff, you're so amazing that I bet you can do both."

I struggled not to roll my eyes.

"I don't want our child around his so-called students," Mike whispered in my ear. "They're probably a bunch of lunatics."

My father must have heard our exchange, because he raised an eyebrow in annoyance. "They're not crazy. These are good, decent folks who happen to love my blog."

"Well, that explains a lot about them," Gianna remarked.

The doorbell sounded. It had to be Brian. I attempted to stand, but my mother put a hand up to stop me. "Stay there, darling. Too much jumping up and down isn't good for the baby." She trotted gaily out of the room, her silver miniskirt winking in the bright lights from the crystal chandelier above the table.

My father watched her leave the room, a proud smile stretched across his round, cherubic face. "Boy, your mother gets hotter every year."

Gianna stifled a groan and put her head back down on her arms, closing her eyes tightly. Johnny watched her anxiously as he reached over to give Alex a spoonful of applesauce. "Maybe we should go," he suggested. "You've had quite a lot to drink, babe."

Gianna's head shot up. "I'm fine. And I want to hear what Brian says. *If* he has anything to say. I swear, that guy still has a crush on Sal."

Mike's arm stiffened around my shoulders at her words, while I did my best not to wince. One never knew what would fall out of the mouth of a drunken Gianna these days. Words spewed forth between her lips like water gushed from a fountain, and it was all I needed right now. Mike had long since considered Brian's infatuation a thing of the past. Gianna was reigniting a fuse with her comments, and I was afraid another world war might break out.

My mother returned to the room with Brian behind her, hat in hand. He nodded to all of us. "Sorry to interrupt your dinner."

"It's no bother." My mother giggled as she sat down and pulled out her compact again from her makeup bag on the table. "We're almost done. Would you like cheesecake and a cup of coffee for dessert?"

"No, thank you." Brian looked uncomfortable when our gazes met. "Uh, Sally, maybe we should talk privately."

My chest tightened with anxiety. "That's not necessary. Whatever you have to say to me you can say in front of my family."

"Jenkins, what's this all about?" Mike demanded. "Did you find something to link Damian to Sal's carjacking? Was he one of the Santas?"

Brian shook his head. "As I told your wife earlier, he wasn't involved in the carjacking."

"What happened to him? Did he overdose?" I asked.

Brian's expression was pained. "No. As you're aware, Sally, we couldn't hold him at the station. He came down of his own free will."

"Why would he do that?" I asked.

He shrugged. "It makes some of those guys feel important, I guess. Or maybe he was willing because he knew the parole officer could prove his innocence. He might have wanted to embarrass us when we found out later that he had an alibi."

"They love to embarrass lawyers too," Gianna added.

Brian pulled a small notepad out of his jacket pocket. "There was a 9-1-1 call placed by his girlfriend, Magnolia Nunez at seven o'clock this evening. She'd spoken to him on the phone at six, so we know the murder happened between that timeframe."

The way Brian watched me was uncomfortable. It wasn't a lovestruck type of look. Suspicion was etched into those chiseled features of his, and I didn't know why. Between six and seven o'clock tonight a man had been murdered—my first high school crush—while I'd dozed on the couch, watched television, and waited for my husband to pick me up for dinner. So what else did this have to do with me?

Brian continued. "Since I recognized the address, I volunteered to take the call. Adam came with me. Magnolia was hysterical and had to be sedated. Damian was lying on his back on the living room floor with his throat cut."

With a shiver, I wrapped my arms protectively around my stomach.

Mike glared at Brian. "There's no need for graphic details. My wife has been through enough the past couple of days. Is that all you had to tell her? Why didn't you do it over the phone?"

"There's more," Brian said. He drew his phone out of his pocket, tapped the screen, and then held it out for us to see. "This is what we found next to Damian's body."

I squinted at the picture and then gasped. Next to Damian's outstretched hand on the floor was a small pink bakery box, lying upended. I could read *Sally's Samples* on the lid. Next to it on the floor was a piece of waxed paper and two of Josie's famous gingerbread cookies. These ones were iced in pink, not the typical white buttercream she always used, but they were definitely her handiwork. She always drew the mouth with one single tooth in the middle. It was her signature trademark, she'd laughingly explained.

Even more disturbing than the cookies was the murder weapon lying next to them. A pink handle caught my eye and a serrated edge tinted with red—blood. My body began to shake with fear as recognition set in.

It was the cake server that Josie had given me yesterday.

CHAPTER SIX

Mike peered over my shoulder at the phone. "What is it?" he asked. "Are those your cookies in the picture?"

"And my cake server," I whispered weakly. "The one I told you about—that Josie gave me as a gift." I stared up at Brian in confusion. "How—no. This is impossible. How could someone have gotten my cake server? Josie was at the bakery until at least six o'clock. It's our busiest time of the year." Oh shoot. Then I remembered her saying that she was closing a half hour earlier tonight. One of her kids had a Christmas concert at school.

A vein bulged in Mike's neck. "Someone is trying to frame you for Damian's murder." He cocked his head in Brian's direction. "Are you sure the server is what killed him?"

Brian nodded. "Positive. Without getting into gory details, it was stuck in the side of his neck. The first thing we did was remove it."

Mike chuckled, and we all glanced at him in amazement. His face colored quickly. "Sorry," he murmured. "I'm not laughing about Damian being killed. It's the idea that Sal had anything to do with it, which is ridiculous. First off, she'd never hurt a fly. Second, she wouldn't have had the strength to plunge that thing into his neck."

Brian eyed my husband thoughtfully for a moment. "If she'd caught him off guard or he'd had his back to her, it's entirely possible. For that matter, anyone could have done this."

My mouth dropped open in shock. "Are you saying you think I killed Damian?"

"Brian, this is ludicrous!" my mother cried.

"Sal, you don't have to answer any questions without a

lawyer present," Gianna chimed in. She burped and then gave a giggle. "Oops. That's right—*I'm* a lawyer."

Jeez Louise. "Brian, you know that I didn't do this." I held my breath and waited for him to answer while the rest of the room grew quiet.

"Yes, I do know," he agreed. "But I don't have any choice in the matter. I have to take you down to the station for questioning."

Mike jumped up from the table. "Like hell you will."

My father pointed a finger at Brian. "For God's sake, you're upsetting her, man. Do you want her to have my grandchild at the police station?"

An overwhelming thought of terror shot through me. What if Brian put me in a holding cell for the night? Maybe I'd go into labor and have to rely on a policeman or a prostitute cellmate to help deliver my baby. Oh. My. God. Why did these things always happen to me?

Mike placed a protective hand on my shoulder. "Sal's staying right here, Jenkins. Look at her, for crying out loud. She's still in shock from what happened last night. Hasn't she been through enough?"

"It's only a formality," Brian said calmly. "Sally's not going to be arrested. Please do me a favor and cooperate. I promise it won't take long, and then you can be on your way home."

Slowly and clumsily, I rose from the table. Mike gently whirled me around to face him. "You don't have to do this, baby." He glared menacingly over my head at Brian. "If anyone thinks you had something to do with this, they're crazy. It's a setup."

"I'm going with you," Gianna announced. She rose from the table, took a step, and tripped over the back of the baby's highchair. Alex started to cry, and Gianna went down in a heap on the carpet.

Johnny was at her side in seconds. "Sweetheart, maybe you overdid it on the wine a little bit."

She looked around for her purse and then gave the baby a kiss on the forehead. "Everything is overdone. Too much stress in my life. Too much weirdness in my family. And our wedding is going to be a chaotic disaster thanks to your grandmother."

My father nodded his approval. "She's right, Johnny. Your grandmother's a nightmare waiting to happen."

Johnny shot my father a surly look but said nothing.

"Wait for me, Sal." Gianna swayed back and forth and then grabbed on to the baby's highchair for support. "Whoops! The room is upside down."

Grandma Rosa spoke in a low but sharp voice. "Gianna, my dear, the only place you are going is to bed. I think that Sally is better off without you."

My father helped himself to a third piece of cheesecake and nodded at Johnny. "Yep. It's all your grandmother's fault. That crazy broad could drive anyone to drink."

He turned his head and spotted Grandma Rosa and Nicoletta standing in the doorway. "Whoops."

Nicoletta's coal black eyes were smoking with anger. "Huh. *You* call *me* crazy? Father Death himself? You the biggest loon in the state. An embarrassment to Italians everywhere." She shook her finger at my mother. "Someday, he gonna put you in one of his coffins. And you still gonna be alive."

My mother burst out laughing. "Oh really, Nicoletta. Domenic's speaking the truth. It's Gianna's wedding. Let her and Johnny do what they want."

"She gotta have an all-Italian wedding," Nicoletta insisted, "or they have bad luck forever. Then the baby grow fat and bald like your husband."

My mother gasped. "What a terrible thing to say! Domenic isn't fat." She ran a hand over his stubbled head. "He's sooo handsome. Why, he's even better looking than George Clooney."

Okay, that was pushing it, but I refrained from comment.

Gianna stumbled toward me, pushing Johnny's hands away. "You see? I told you we should have eloped. This wedding has *Titanic* written all over it."

"Excuse me?" Mike raised his voice to be heard above the commotion. "We seem to have a more important matter here to deal with now. My wife is being accused of murder."

"Bah, what you say." Nicoletta sat down and helped herself to a piece of cake. "That nothing new."

Brian's nostrils flared as he and Mike stared each other down. "I told you she hasn't been accused of anything yet."

"Sal…" Gianna slurred her speech, and my name sounded like *Shall.* "Don't worry. I'll defend you."

"You're drunk as a skunk," my father protested and gestured at Johnny. "You might be Italian, son, but you sure don't know how to handle your woman."

"Domenic!" Maria cried. "You apologize to Gianna and Johnny right now."

I shut my eyes and almost started to click my heels, wishing I could disappear. What I'd always been afraid of for years was finally happening. My crazy, wild ride of a family was about to fall over the cliff.

My father threw his arms open wide and looked apologetic. "Hey, I'm just speaking the truth, hot stuff. Our daughter is a well-respected lawyer, but right now she's acting like a common drunk. If she goes with Sal, all three of them will wind up in the slammer, our grandchild included."

"That is enough," Grandma Rosa said sharply. "You all sound like a bunch of clowns." She touched Johnny's arm. "You take Gianna home. She cannot go to the police station with Sally. It is not good for Sally, and it is not good for Gianna. If someone Gianna works with sees her acting like a rhino, she may get into trouble."

Gianna looked at my grandmother in horror. "What did you just call me?"

"Um, that's *wino*, Grandma," I whispered.

"That is good too," she agreed. "Mike, you and Sally go with Brian. Brian will not let anything happen to her tonight. And as for you," she addressed my father. "Sit down and eat your cake. You are always causing trouble. Eat until you burst, and then go write your *pazza* blog."

My father mumbled under his breath but did as he was told.

Nicoletta started to jump up and down with excitement. Her black coat flailed out around her sticklike frame, making her look a bit like the grim reaper. "Yes, he is a loon. I think—"

"Don't think," Grandma Rosa interrupted and pointed to the door. "Time for the rest of the crazies to go home and go to bed."

"I never be so insulted," Nicoletta grumbled.

"Yes, you have," Grandma Rosa said. "Are we still on for cards tomorrow night?"

"Yeah yeah," Nicoletta agreed. "But *you* gotta bring the chips and salsa this time." She grunted at all of us, and a moment later we heard the kitchen door bang shut behind her.

Mike placed my coat around my shoulders. "Come on, princess. Let's get this over with. Are we allowed to take our own car, officer? Or maybe you'd like to handcuff my wife and put her in your backseat?"

Gianna giggled as Johnny led her out of the room. "He's probably thought about it numerous times."

Heat flooded my cheeks, and the room grew so quiet that you could have heard one of Nicoletta's hairpins drop. When I dared to look at Brian, he turned and walked out of the room.

"I'll meet you both outside," he called over his shoulder. "Mike, you can follow me in your own car."

"I'll bring Alex out to yours, Gianna," my mother said as Johnny handed Gianna her coat, and they left the room. Never mind the baby, poor Johnny had his hands full with my sister alone.

My mother strapped the sleeping child into his car seat and trotted after them. Alex was a true mystery to me. He cried when it was quiet and slept when it was noisy. Maybe Gianna should let him live at my parents' house. She'd never hear a peep out of him again.

My father poured himself another glass of wine. "Good luck, baby girl. Hey, keep your eyes open for any interesting goings-on at the police station. I need a new subject for the blog tomorrow."

"My God," Mike exploded as we walked onto the front porch with my grandmother behind us. "Just when I think your family can't get any weirder, something like this happens."

Grandma Rosa kissed me on the cheek, and I clung to her tightly for a moment. "It's all a mistake, isn't it?" My voice quavered as I spoke into her shoulder. "Maybe someone else has a server like mine." With the same engraving? *Property of Baker Sally Donovan.* Right. Oh yeah, that could definitely happen.

She sighed and patted my back. "I would like to think so, *cara mia*. But this is *you* we are talking about, remember."

* * *

Twenty minutes later Mike and I were seated in the police station's interrogation room. Perhaps I'd jinxed myself earlier, recalling how I'd never been in there before. Maybe I'd jinxed myself by getting out of bed this morning—who knew?

It was a sparse room with a small wooden table and two black plastic chairs stationed on either side. The chairs, I noticed, were bolted to the floor. After being involved in almost a dozen murders, I'd finally reached full criminal status.

Brian nodded toward the DVD recorder in the center of the table. "I hope you don't mind that I'm recording this. It's standard procedure."

Mike held my hand tightly and shot him a death glare. "She really doesn't have any choice, does she, Jenkins?"

Brian gritted his teeth in exasperation. "Look, Mike. I'm doing you a favor by letting you stay in the room with Sally. I could have told you to wait in the hallway. Now, if I hear one more word out of you, that's where you're headed."

I shifted uneasily in my seat, watching the body language of the two men as they observed each other in silence. This was all I needed right now—a battle of wills between two very stubborn men. Gianna's comment about Brian being interested in me hadn't gone unnoticed by Mike either. It didn't help the current situation, but this wasn't jealousy on his part. He was angry about the way Brian was treating me—like a common criminal, as he'd pointed out on our drive over here.

"Mike." I tried to sound more confident than I felt. "I'd really like you to stay, so let me answer the questions, okay? It's not like I have anything to hide. The sooner I'm done, the sooner we can go home."

Mike's rigid body relaxed a bit, and he drew my hand to his mouth, still glaring at Brian. "You're right. I'm sorry, princess. This is a lot for you to go through, especially right now. Okay, I'll stay quiet. Promise."

"Good," Brian muttered as he jotted something down on

a piece of paper. "Sally, do you know what time the bakery closed tonight?"

My eyebrows drew together. "Well, it's usually six o'clock at this time of year, but Josie had another obligation and had to leave at five thirty."

He cocked an eyebrow at me. "I've already placed a call to have Josie come down for questioning but haven't heard back from her yet."

I stared at him in disbelief. "That's probably because she's at her son's school for a Christmas concert. I doubt she's answering her phone for anyone."

"Well, I'll go to her house later if I have to," he replied grimly.

This was too much. "Brian, you know that neither Josie nor I had anything to do with Damian's murder. Why would we kill him? Someone must have broken into the shop to steal the cake server."

He ignored my comment. "What were you doing between five thirty and seven o'clock?"

"I was at home, waiting for Mike. When he arrived, we left for my parents' house."

Brian calmly looked over at Mike. "And you got home at what time?"

Mike paused to think. "Six thirty? I may be a minute or two off though, so don't hold that against us." His tone dripped with sarcasm.

Brian tapped a pen against his perfect white teeth. "So, you were alone for about an hour, Sally?"

I didn't like what he was implying. "I was alone all afternoon, but—"

"Just answer the question please," Brian said curtly.

Mike shot him a death glare, but mercifully said nothing. The tension in the room was so thick that you could cut it with a cake server. I shuddered at the thought. "Yes, I was alone between five thirty and six thirty. Well, except for Spike, but for some reason I don't think he's going to confirm my statement."

Brian's jaw dropped at my sarcastic comment, and I was surprised myself. I always tried to cooperate with the law, but I didn't enjoy being questioned like I was a felon.

Brian leaned back in his chair and studied me. "The fact remains that you were alone for an hour. Damian only lives ten minutes from your house."

Mike's eyes glittered. "What are you trying to say?"

"I told you not to interfere in my questioning." Brian jerked his thumb toward the door. "Outside, please."

"Forget it. I'm not leaving." Mike folded his arms across his chest and remained seated.

"You promised not to say anything else!" I chided my husband and then looked imploringly at Brian. "You know that I didn't kill him."

Brian switched the recorder off. He rose from his chair, and we followed suit. "I can't take this anymore, Sally. I'm going to ask to be removed from this investigation." He ran an agitated hand through his hair. "I'm too close to both of you to be objective. If further questioning is needed, another officer will be assigned."

Great. Wonderful. My only ally was gone. I'd come to depend on Brian in difficult situations and wondered what would happen to me next. Fear knotted in the pit of my stomach. Damian and I had a past together. Okay, it was 16 years ago, and the entire idea was ridiculous, but it was still a past. His address had shown up in my vehicle after I'd been carjacked and had a gun held to my head. My serrated cake server had been found next to his dead body, along with my gingerbread cookies. How was anyone going to believe that I *hadn't* killed him?

If everyone in town found out I was a suspect, it would make business in the shop nonexistent. I knew that Mike was worried the stress might affect my health and the baby's. I gripped his hand tightly as Brian held the office door open for us. "No one's going to find out about this, right?"

"Don't worry," Brian assured me. "It's strictly confidential. Besides, it wouldn't be a good thing if the media did find out. They always seem to have a field day at your expense, Sally."

Boy, he wasn't kidding. My bakery had been referred to as Sally's Shambles many times, thanks to the dead bodies I somehow always managed to stumble across.

A woman about my age was sitting on the wooden bench

in the hall, wiping her eyes with a tissue. Despite the cold night, she was dressed in a sleeveless one-piece black halter dress with sequins and matching sandals. A black leather jacket was draped over the arm of the bench. Her angular face was heavily made up, and her shoulder-length dark hair was tousled and messy. She looked up, and our eyes met, recognition instantly setting in for both of us.

"Magnolia?" I asked.

Magnolia Nunez had been a high school classmate of mine, the girl Damian had thrown me over for. They'd dated off and on through high school and the following years, but at my ten-year reunion, they'd both attended with different dates. The latest rumor in Colwestern was that they were back on again. Magnolia had found his body, so she must be here for questioning.

Adam, who had been at the front counter talking to another officer, came over and nodded at us before addressing Magnolia. "Right this way, Miss Nunez, and we'll get a statement from you."

"Sally Muccio." Magnolia's voice was full of venom. "This is all your fault."

Bewildered, I stared at her. "What are you talking about?"

"Miss Nunez." Adam touched her lightly on the arm. "I said to follow me please."

She shook him off and pointed a blood red acrylic nail at my face. "Damian told me all about you. You accused him of carjacking you. Guess you wanted to even the score, huh?"

Mike stepped between us. "You're crazy. My wife had nothing to do with his death. Stop harassing her."

She licked her lips, same color as her nails, and laughed. "Oh, that's right. I heard you two got married. Probably because she couldn't have Damian."

There had to be something in Colwestern's water. There was no other explanation for why anyone could think that I was still obsessed with the man after all these years.

Mike's body stiffened against mine. "Yeah, right. Get this through your head, Magnolia. Sally wasn't interested in your drug-dealing boyfriend. In fact, she's been through hell thanks to him."

    Magnolia gasped. "Been through *what?* She's the one who killed him." Tears flooded her eyes as she lunged toward me. "I hope you rot in hell."

CHAPTER SEVEN

———

I shut my eyes tightly and prayed that the past 24 hours had been a dream. When I opened them again, I'd be lying in a hospital bed with our beautiful baby in my arms and Mike by my side. Perhaps carolers would even be outside the window. I'd heard that they visited hospitals during the Christmas season. *Oh, please let this all be a dream.*

Hopeful, I opened my eyes. No such luck. I was sitting on the bench discarded by Magnolia a moment ago. The bad dream had become a nightmare of reality, one that there was no waking from.

Adam had managed to restrain Magnolia before she reached me. We watched as she was led into the interrogation room, which was doing a booming business today. Magnolia continued to shout obscenities at me until Adam pushed her in ahead of him and slammed the door shut.

"You okay?" Brian asked me.

I managed a nod as Mike's arm went around my shoulders. "A little shaken."

He leaned against the wall. "Magnolia was in school with you and Damian?"

"Yes, but I didn't know her well. Magnolia's sister Dru Ann was in the same class as Gianna, and they were friendly to each other. She comes into the bakery occasionally. Last time Dru Ann was in, she told Josie that Damian and Magnolia were back together, but Magnolia thought he was dating his ex behind her back."

"That would be Rachel Hedley." Brian studied a paper in front of him. "She works at Colwestern Mall as a hairdresser. She's next on my list to question. It's interesting how both women showed up at his apartment last night." He shook his head, as if trying to absorb it all. "They don't get along, of course. Magnolia had to be restrained when she saw Rachel. A cat fight waiting to happen. Earlier, Magnolia told Adam that Damian mentioned he'd run into you."

"So that's it," Mike said with fury. "Magnolia killed him, and she framed Sal."

Brian held up a hand. "We don't have any proof that's what happened."

Although Brian didn't say it out loud, there certainly seemed to be plenty of proof on hand that *I* had done the deed. "This is insane. Dru Ann also told Josie that Damian's ex had a former drug problem, and the family blamed Damian for getting her hooked."

"Let's not forget how he turned up stoned at our ten-year reunion." Mike pursed his lips. "Then he started a fight with another classmate, and the police had to be called."

"I'm familiar with his past record," Brian said dryly. "Like I said earlier, he's been clean since last summer. He told his parole officer last night that he'd had a wake-up call."

I wondered what that meant.

"Forget about him," Mike interrupted. "Look, I'm sorry the guy is dead, but my wife is not responsible, and you know it, Brian. Can I take her home now?"

He nodded. "Yes, but make sure that you stay close by if we have further questions."

Mike swore under his breath while I choked back a laugh. "Brian, will you look at me please? Where would I go when I'm about to have a baby any minute?"

Before he could reply, the front door to the station opened, and Josie walked in. Her blue eyes went wide with alarm when she caught sight of us, and she rushed over.

"I came as soon as I got Brian's message," she said. "What's going on? Sal, why are you guys here? Did the Santas show up again?"

"No. Damian's dead."

She brought a hand to her mouth. "Holy crap. What happened?"

Poor Josie was going to feel responsible when I told her

about the cake server, so I needed to be delicate. "He was stabbed in the neck, and it looks like it may have been done with my cake server—the one you gave me yesterday."

To my surprise, she slapped herself in the forehead. "Oh man! I should have called the police. This is all my fault."

Puzzled, we all stared at her. "Your fault?" I asked.

"Do you know how the server wound up in his apartment?" Brian inquired.

Josie blew out a long, steady breath. "No, but I stopped at the bakery after Danny's concert, before I came here. I'd taken my own car to the school, so Rob took the kids home without me. I'd forgotten my phone at the bakery and didn't have time to go back and grab it before the show. When I went into the back room, the alarm didn't go off." She lowered her eyes in embarrassment. "I asked Dodie to lock up because I was in a hurry, and she must have forgotten to set the alarm. This is all my fault, Sal."

Now I wanted to slap *myself* in the forehead. We forgot to set the alarm for one day, and a break-in occurred. Yes, it could only happen to us. "Did you find anything missing?"

Josie shook her head. "I didn't even think to check for the server. But when I grabbed my phone off the display case—" She paused. "Oh, never mind. I'm sure it had nothing to do with Damian."

"What did you notice? Come on, Jos," I urged. "Anything might help."

She frowned. "Well, there were some gingerbread men left in the case before I closed up. When I stopped back after the concert, they were gone. I thought Dodie might have taken them or maybe you'd stopped to grab them on the way to your parents."

"No, I didn't go near the shop today. Damian's killer must have taken them when they stole the server."

Josie addressed Brian. "I know that the server was there this morning, because one of our customers made a comment about it. So that should clear Sal."

Brian looked pained. "Sally's not under arrest. If someone IDs her going into Damian's building earlier tonight or if she's spotted on the surveillance camera, then that's a different story."

"It's ridiculous that she even had to come here," Mike muttered, obviously wanting to have the last word.

Brian ignored his comment and showed Josie the picture of the crime scene on his phone. "Did you make these cookies?"

She nodded solemnly. "I decided to use up the leftover strawberry icing I had on hand for them. I thought they looked cute, but everyone asked for gingerbread men with white icing. Go figure. I planned to sell them at half price tomorrow. Boy, I won't make that mistake again. Good thing there was only about a dozen of them."

"Does anyone else know about the cookies?" I quaked at the thought. It felt like another strike against my innocence. Damian had told Magnolia about the carjacking. Who else had he told? He'd clearly enjoyed the attention, because he'd willingly come to the station when Brian asked him to. "Does Magnolia have an alibi? What if she killed him?"

Brian narrowed his eyes. "Don't even go there, Sally. Stay out of this."

"How do you expect me to stay out of this?" I shrieked. "I'm a murder suspect!"

The cop behind the front desk and the woman he was speaking to both looked over at us. *Way to fly under the radar, Sal.*

Brian turned to Mike. "Take her home." His gaze met mine for a brief second, and then he looked away. "If you have questions tomorrow, please talk to Adam. Or my boss, Sergeant Graves. Anyone but me."

* * *

It was another night of tossing and turning for me. I experienced some Braxton Hicks contractions and was almost convinced it was the real thing, but they'd stopped all of a sudden. Too bad. Labor and back pain sounded more pleasant than prison.

The sun dawned brightly the next morning, radiating the cloudless sky, but it did nothing to help my current sour mood. My fitting for Gianna's wedding was rescheduled for tonight, and that only depressed me further. After Mike left for work, I took a shower and drove to my doctor's appointment. There were no signs of labor in progress, so Dr. Chandler scheduled me for another appointment on Tuesday morning, which was also Christmas Eve. I'd already explained about Gianna's wedding, but he wanted me to come in anyway.

As soon as I returned home, I put my pajamas back on and got into bed, then proceeded to watch three straight hours of game shows and soap operas. I'd also turned my phone off, an attempt to shut off the real world for a while.

Maybe the pregnancy was affecting my brain. I shouldn't be depressed. For goodness' sake, I was having a baby—the biggest thrill of my life. But my excitement had been temporarily dulled due to the fact that I was a potential murder suspect. Brian refused to help me, so I was on my own.

At two o'clock, I got out of bed and turned my phone back on. It rang within seconds. Mike was calling, and he sounded upset. "Sal, I've been texting you for the last two hours! I was about ready to drive over. I thought something had happened to you."

My shoulders sagged. I'd done it again, caused him more unnecessary worry. "Sorry, honey. I needed a break, so I shut it off. Guess I wasn't thinking."

His voice grew soft. "I hate that this is happening to you. Did the police call about further questioning?"

"Not yet. Hey, no news is good news, right?" I tried to sound lighthearted, but couldn't hide my feelings from him. Mike knew me too well.

"If they ask you to come down to the station," Mike continued, "call me right away. You are not going by yourself. Promise me, baby."

"Of course. I promise." His remark made me more irritated at Brian. I'd tried to be sympathetic to his situation last night, but if he'd needed my help, *I* wouldn't have deserted *him*. Then again, his personal situation might be playing a part. He and Ally had squabbled more than enough over me in the past.

"Gianna will be here soon," I went on. "She's leaving work early, and we're both having a last-minute fitting. If you don't hear from me for a while, please don't worry. I'll be struggling to get into my tent."

He chuckled on the other end. "I know that you think you've gained a little weight—"

"A *little*?" Incredulity filled my voice. "You're trying to be nice, but let's face the facts here. I'm a butterball."

His voice was gentle and barely above a whisper. "You've never looked more beautiful to me. Before you started carrying our child, I didn't think it was possible to love you more. But I was wrong."

Tears flooded my eyes. Damn hormones. I'd always cried easily, but the last couple of months I'd become a regular waterfall. "You did it again," I sobbed.

"What now?" he sounded puzzled.

I blew my nose into a tissue. "You keep making me cry."

Mike laughed out loud. "It won't be much longer, princess. Hang in there. Trust me. It will all be worth it once you see that little face."

His words made my heart melt. "I can't wait."

"Me either," Mike said. "Love you."

"Love you too."

As I waited for Gianna, I absorbed myself with repositioning some of the ornaments on our seven-foot fir Christmas tree. I inhaled the rich pine smell and stared mesmerized at the twinkling lights. I lovingly fingered the *Baby's First Christmas* rocking horse ornament Gianna had given me at my baby shower last month. My heart soared when I imagined holding my precious little bundle of joy. I'd been certain the baby would arrive before Christmas, but now I was starting to wonder if that would happen.

A horn tooted from outside. I glanced out the bay window and spotted Gianna's car in the driveway. I grabbed my purse, set the alarm, and locked the door. The weather was warm for this time of year, about 45 degrees, and a generous amount of snow had melted as a result. Although unusual, it made navigating the outdoors much easier for me.

Gianna drove in silence for a few minutes, then stole a sideways glance at me. "Sal, I'm sorry about last night. I was a complete idiot and way out of line."

I reached over to squeeze her hand. "No worries. And it

wasn't so bad. Brian only asked me a few questions and even let Mike stay. It would have been a waste of your time."

Her lower lip trembled. "That's not the point. When someone is in trouble, especially a member of my own family, it's my job to defend them. I let you down." She paused for a moment before continuing. "I let everyone down these days. I can't plan a wedding or take decent care of my baby. Now I can't even do my job." A lone tear rolled down her cheek.

"Stop it. None of that is true. You're a wonderful mother and a terrific lawyer. Don't beat yourself up over it." I hated to see her like this.

Gianna was quiet for a few minutes, and it bothered me. Finally, I spoke up. "Gi, I hate to ask, but is everything okay between you and Johnny?"

She nodded and turned into the parking lot of Becky's Bridals. "Johnny's a true Mr. Mom. He's with the baby all day, you know, and they've really bonded. Alex is wonderful with his father, but he cries constantly whenever I watch him. He's even great when Nicoletta babysits him. Go figure. You know that she's driving me insane."

"She drives everyone insane. It's her job."

Gianna blew out a breath as she parked the car. "She insisted on inviting several friends of hers to the wedding—people that Johnny and I don't even know. I don't mean to be a jerk about the financial part, but other than the money Mom and Dad have contributed for the limousine and disc jockey, Johnny and I are footing the rest of the bill. Nicoletta hasn't given us one dime, yet she still expects to call all the shots."

"It's that Sicilian nature of hers." I sighed.

"I know Nicoletta's been through a lot with her health and Johnny's mother dying so young, but jeez! She needs to stay out of our lives. And it isn't just a Sicilian thing. Grandma's never acted like that."

"Grandma's one in a million, remember. Don't you dare let Nicoletta spoil everything. It's your and Johnny's day, and you should do whatever you want. Mike and I will do anything we can to support you both."

"Thanks, Sal." She gave me a wistful smile. "Honestly, I wish we had eloped. I love the idea of a Christmas wedding, but it's too much, especially with Alex teething and Nicoletta's interfering. Not to mention it's the worst time ever for you. I thought you might go a week or two early, like me. I feel so bad about putting you through this."

I heaved myself out of the car. "It's all right. Maybe the baby will come before the wedding. Hopefully, not while I'm walking down the aisle."

"Oh, no big deal," she assured me. "You always manage to get yourself out of difficult situations, so what's one more?" She looped her arm through mine as we headed for the entrance.

Becky's Bridals was the same boutique I'd gotten my wedding gown. There were other bridal stores in Colwestern, but this one was by far the best. The shop was situated in a duplex, with one side as Becky's business and the other her personal residence. We knew Becky Winchester personally since she'd been a former classmate of my mother's.

The building itself was cute as a button—white, vinyl siding adorned by pink shutters and a large sign with hot pink letters that read, *Be a Becky Bride and Put Some Romance in Your Life.* Inside of the salon was even more adorable with pale pink walls and rose-colored carpeting. The salon was split into two rooms, a similar setup to my bakery. One room contained racks of wedding gowns in almost every color, while the other was devoted to bridesmaids, mother of the bride, and in-law gowns.

"There they are!" Becky yelled to her daughter, Lydia, one of the seamstresses. "The Muccio girls have arrived. Okay, the Donovan and soon-to-be Gavelli wives, if you want to get technical. But you'll always be Muccio at heart. Come on into the dressing rooms. We're ready for you."

Becky was loud, brash, and good at her job. She'd been divorced three times, knew everyone's business in Colwestern, and in return, everyone knew hers. Like my mother, she had a fantastic figure and wore as little clothing as possible. Today she was wearing, of all things, a mini Santa dress and hat with knee-high black leather boots. It looked great on her but made me cringe. Lately I'd seen enough of Santa to last me a lifetime.

"Lydia's ready for you, doll," she said to Gianna as she led me to a dressing room. My gown, a red silk creation with short, puffy sleeves was already in there waiting for me. Becky patted my belly. "When are you due again?"

"Two days ago," I said.

Her mouth dropped open in surprise. "Oh, honey. I hope your water doesn't break while you're walking down the aisle. I can't imagine anything worse."

Sadly, I could—having my baby in a prison cell, for starters. The very thought sent another tremor of fear through my body.

"You're shaking like a leaf, honey." Becky snapped her gum in my ear as she adjusted the sleeves of the dress. "Don't worry. If it's too tight, we can let it out again." She stood back and studied me critically. "How does it feel?" She started to pluck the material around my waist. "Oops. No room there. That's all baby."

"It's a bit snug," I confessed. Ugh. I didn't want to come back for another fitting. Becky was wrong. There wasn't enough material in the entire world to fit me. I managed a small laugh. "But I won't get any bigger in a couple of days, right?"

She smoothed out a wrinkle in the skirt. "They say that the baby gains half a pound every week in the last month of pregnancy. I was smaller than you, and Lydia weighed ten pounds. No one, not even the doctor, thought she'd weigh that much. They had to use forceps, and she still didn't want to leave." Becky giggled. "Then after twenty hours of agonizing labor, I had to have a C-section."

Becky wasn't cheering me up any. I was done with hearing about other women's pregnancy tales. Every mother in the world had one, and at my baby shower I'd been regaled with them. Each story had been worse than the previous one.

Becky helped me change back into my sweatpants and T-shirt and placed the dress in a garment bag. "If you change your mind, we can always have another fitting, hon. And if the baby comes before the wedding—" She frowned thoughtfully. "Well, we'll think of something."

I emerged from the dressing room to find Gianna standing in front of the three-way floor-to-ceiling mirror, studying herself critically from each angle. She was stunning in an antique veil and tulle and lace dress. The bodice had embroidered appliques and beading, while the long sleeves with floral motifs gave it a very romantic look. I'd seen her in the dress before, but she still managed to blow me away with her natural beauty.

My eyes started to tear as I looked at her. My baby sister was getting married. "You look more beautiful every time you try it on."

Her cheeks flushed pink at the compliment. "Thanks, Sal. I needed to hear that today."

Lydia fluffed out the delicate skirt. "One of our customers who was in this morning said that a Muccio girl had her picture in the paper! Must be our bride-to-be."

"Oh!" Becky said excitedly. "There's one at the front counter. I haven't looked at it yet. I'll bring it right back." She hurried to the front of the store.

"It must be the engagement photo. They certainly took their time!" Gianna said indignantly. "The *Colwestern Journal* promised it would be in two weeks ago."

Becky returned within a minute, but she was no longer smiling. She stared down at the paper between her slim hands, then looked hesitantly at me.

My heart gave a jolt of fear. "What's wrong?"

She swallowed hard, her eyes troubled as they locked on to mine. "I guess they meant you and not Gianna, honey."

Becky held out the paper, and having no choice, I grabbed it. Sure enough, there I was, front page center, leaving the police station last night with Mike's arm around me. Above the picture and caption was Jerry Maroon's name in bold italic letters, followed by the headline *Local Business Owner Bakes Up a Murder.*

CHAPTER EIGHT

———

"This is an outrage!" Gianna cried as she drove away from the shop. "I'm going to have that Maroon's job. Hasn't he caused you enough trouble already?"

I leaned my head back against the seat in disgust. Just when I thought things couldn't get any worse. "Take me to the bakery please."

She shot me a funny look. "I thought you were done working."

"Well, it's still my shop, and I need to talk to Josie. I'll catch a ride home with her."

Gianna hesitated. "Sal, I know what you're thinking. Please don't do it."

"I have no choice. This article is going to be bad for business because now everyone will think that I killed Damian."

"They're your faithful customers," Gianna said. "Do you really think they'd believe a nine-month pregnant woman slit some drug dealer's throat?"

We both exchanged a knowing look and sighed. This was Colwestern. People believed whatever was in the newspaper and in blogs like my father's. In short, I was doomed.

"Maybe it won't be so bad," she remarked. "Brian knows you're not a criminal. He won't let you be arrested."

"Brian's removing himself from the case. He said this is too personal for him."

She glanced at me sharply, but to my relief, didn't provide a wisecrack. "Then I think you should let the department handle it. I know you've solved some tricky cases in the past, but this time is different. You're not in any condition to go snooping around. It's dangerous for you and the baby."

"I know this. The baby's welfare comes first, and I'm not about to do anything stupid that might hurt him or her. I only want to have a talk with Rachel, Damian's ex, and see if she knows anything. Maybe she had something to do with his death. If he dumped her to go back to Magnolia, she might have a motive to kill him."

Gianna shook her head in disgust. "This is what I don't understand. What was so great about the guy? He was a drug user. I remember Damian from high school, even though I was three years behind you guys. He was good looking, but so what? The man was no prize. He was always getting called into the principal's office. I checked into his priors today. Drug busts, assault, even a domestic dispute. Would they honestly have pulled the 'If I can't have you, no one can' card with this loser?"

I shrugged. "Who knows? Stranger things could happen."

She considered this for a moment. "Yeah, you do know all about that."

If Gianna was trying to make me feel better, she was failing miserably at the task. "Look. Someone killed Damian and is framing me. Why, I don't know. But if a person, say Magnolia, goes to the cops and says they saw me at his apartment that night, I'm done for."

"It won't happen." Gianna was lying through her teeth, but I went along with it. She pulled her car into the alley behind the bakery. "If you need me, I won't let you down again. That's a promise. I'm headed back to my office, and the first thing I'm going to do is file a complaint against Jerry Maroon."

"Don't do it yet," I pleaded. "I'd like to find out who his source is first." The article, unlike the headline, didn't come right out and say I had killed Damian. Good old Jerry was being extra careful about his wording these days. The article explained that I was the number one suspect and had been brought in for questioning. He also knew that my cake server had been used as the murder weapon. I was dumbfounded. The police hadn't disclosed the weapon's details, so where was Jerry getting his information from?

"All right. But say the word, and I'll have that guy on

slander charges. Now take care of yourself and Alex's future playmate." She pulled me into a hug before I lumbered out of the car and waved as she drove away.

I inserted my key into the doorknob that led to the kitchen workspace area. As I pushed it open, I heard a bang followed by a shriek. Dodie stood there, looking miserable, with a tray of broken gingerbread at her feet.

She placed a hand over her heart. "Oh, Sally, I'm so sorry. You startled me." She kneeled down and started to clean up the mess. "You can take it out of my paycheck. It won't happen again. I promise."

"Dodie, watch out—"

She straightened up from the floor and promptly banged her head against the block table while I winced inwardly.

"Oh my God. Are you all right?"

Dodie took her hand away from her forehead, where a huge lump was already forming. "I'm fine," she mumbled. "Guess I'm having a bad day."

From what I'd seen, Dodie didn't have many good days. It was hard not to watch her episodes of daily clumsiness without wondering how much this was costing me in profits. Maybe my accountant would let me write her off as a loss next year.

I was starting to think that Dodie was some kind of a jinx. Still, it was impossible not to like her. The sixty-something-year-old woman with silver hair and gray eyes had a very sweet disposition, and she enjoyed entertaining customers and me with stories about her eight grandchildren. She'd been widowed for ten years and had confided to me that baking was a happy way for her to fill the long, often empty days. Dodie understood this might only be a temporary job for her as I attempted to find a way to juggle both bakery and baby, and she was fine with that. Her late husband had left her a sizeable life insurance policy, so whatever the outcome, she'd be okay.

Josie hurried in from the storefront. "What's all the commotion back here?" She looked down at the broken cookies that Dodie was hastily piling back onto the tray and sucked in some air. "Oh. I see the problem."

"I had a little accident," Dodie said sheepishly.

Josie raised her eyebrows. "Dodie, it's almost five

o'clock. Why don't you head on home early?"

Dodie looked uncertain. "Shouldn't I stay and help clean up the—"

"No!" Josie spoke a bit more loudly than she'd intended. "I mean, nope, it's all good. I'll see you tomorrow."

Dodie beamed while she put on her coat. "Okay, girls. Have a lovely night, and Sally, if I don't see you tomorrow, I'm betting that sweet baby comes before Monday. You know, I have a very good instinct about these things." She gave us a little finger wave, turned, then bumped into the closed door. "Oops. Guess I forgot it wasn't open." She stumbled out into the night and caught her scarf in the door. She reopened it, removed the scarf, then meekly shut the door again.

Josie slumped against the worktable. "I'm not sure how much more of this I can take, Sal. She's a walking disaster. Not that it mattered today though."

Perplexed, I stared at her. "What do you mean?"

She walked over to the sink and began to wash the few dishes stacked in it while I grabbed a sponge to wipe down the worktable. "It means that we started off great, and then business started to dry up during the day until there was no one left in the store. I don't understand what happened."

Uh-oh. It had started already. I twisted the sponge between my hands. "I think it's my fault. Have you seen the *Colwestern Journal* today?"

Josie narrowed her blue eyes. "Oh no. You're in the paper *again?* Is it about Damian's murder?"

I spread my hands out wide in a dramatic fashion. "Yep. You win the door prize. Good old Jerry Maroon snapped a picture of me leaving the police station last night with Mike. The article said I was the police's top suspect."

"That son of a—" Josie's face turned as red as her hair. "Good God, Sal. This is turning into a nightmare for you!"

"What really hurts me is that our customers believe I could have done such a thing." Some of them had been coming in almost daily since we opened the doors. "They know me— they joke around with us. How can they think that I killed someone?"

Josie's expression was grim. "The problem is that these

days anyone can commit a murder—from a ten-year-old kid to a ninety-year-old grandmother. How many times do you watch the news and see someone talking about the nice woman who lived across the street? 'We babysat each other's kids. I'd never suspect her of being a killer.' You've been involved in so many murder cases that maybe people are starting to look at you in a different way."

How ironic. I'd been calling Dodie a jinx, but the fact of the matter was that I was the cursed one. Josie had made a logical point. If I knew someone who always had a habit of getting involved in a murder investigation or finding dead bodies, would I think there was something ominous about her?

Yes, I probably would.

I sat down on a stool in an attempt to relieve my aching back. It didn't work. "Since Brian is out of the picture, I'll have to try to find the killer myself. And because of my current condition, I need your help more than ever."

Josie's mouth dropped open in surprise. "Of course. We're a team! But Brian won't desert you. He'll come around."

"I'm not so sure. Either way, we need to work fast. I thought maybe we could start by talking to Damian's ex-girlfriend. Her name is Rachel Hedley, and she works at the Colwestern Mall as a hairdresser."

Josie glanced at her watch. "Dru Ann mentioned her name, but I'd forgotten it until now. All right. For some strange reason, I don't think we're getting any more customers today, so let's close up." She hurried out front to lock the door and put the *Closed* sign on. "What's the name of the place she works at? The mall's open late for Christmas, but I believe the hair salons always close at six."

I set the alarm, shut the lights off, and locked the door behind Josie as we made our way to her minivan. "Isn't there only one—the Hair or There place? I hope she's working today."

Josie started the engine. "Think positive. Rob's working tonight, so I need to be home close to my regular time."

"We won't stay long. I'd rather not mention it to Mike, if I can help it. He'll be upset."

Josie's blue eyes were anxious. "Well, I can't say I blame him. You're going to have that baby any second."

My voice trembled. "Yes, and I don't want it to be in a jail cell. This is also our busiest time of the year, and we can't afford to lose any money. Let's face it—this hasn't exactly been a banner year."

She patted my arm. "I know. With Mike getting injured and out of work last spring, you guys have had a tough time financially. But I have a feeling next year is going to be your best yet. It has to be, because your little angel will be here, right? You've waited so long for this, Sal. No one deserves it more than you."

"Sometimes I feel like I've been waiting for this baby my entire life." I rubbed my belly gently and smiled at the colorful holiday lights that surrounded the mall's exterior. Strands from *Rudolph the Red Nosed Reindeer* drifted through the air from a set of building speakers while Santa's sleigh and eight toy reindeer were parked by the main entrance. Luckily, we found a parking spot close by. A Santa Claus was ringing a Salvation Army bell, and he smiled at us. I stopped to extract a couple of dollar bills from my wallet. He nodded in approval as I dropped the money into his red kettle. "Merry Christmas, ma'am. Ho ho ho!"

Ugh. I managed a small smile for him but doubted those words would ever have the same appeal again.

As we walked in the direction of Hair or There, I caught sight of a sign displayed over the directory. *Come and meet Santa at Guest Services! Every day until Christmas Eve, from 3:00 to 6:00 p.m.*

Josie gave a snort. "My kids would never fall for that."

"They don't believe in Santa anymore?" I asked.

"Danny doesn't," Josie said. "Dylan is on the fence, but my little two are still heavily into the big red man. What I meant is, if they saw all the Santas in here, they'd start asking questions, and the self-doubt would kick in. My kids don't fall for the 'they're all Santa's helpers' bit."

"That's because they're no-nonsense like their mother," I teased. "How many Santas are usually here on a given day?"

"It varies," Josie said. "I was shopping last week with my mother-in-law and spotted at least five Santas. Kids aren't stupid. Hey, has Gianna brought Alex to see Santa yet?"

"Gianna hasn't had time to breathe lately," I murmured, "but I do think they were planning to try to come tomorrow." A light switch clicked on in my brain. "Where do you think these Santas get their costumes from?"

Josie shrugged. "Well, there's the holiday costume store over on Starwood Avenue. I think it's the only one in town." She snapped her fingers. "Oh! Are you thinking that maybe the Jolly-less Santas suits came from there?"

"Doubtful," I conceded. "They were kind of cheap looking. And the Santas would have to be pretty stupid if they bought the suits locally, wouldn't they?"

"From what you've told me, they didn't seem like the brightest bulbs in the box. Didn't you say they might have been street kids and that Brian thought they lived nearby? Hey, I was a street kid once too."

I shot her a look of disbelief. "No, you weren't. You hung out with *me.*"

"Yes, but I also spent time on the street." Josie's expression sobered. "My parents didn't care who I hung out with. They couldn't keep track of all of us and didn't even want to. I know that your mother and father are about as weird as they can get, but I'd give my right arm to have parents who care about me the way they care about you and Gianna. And of course, no one compares to your grandmother. Not to make excuses, but if I'd had people in my life like that, maybe I would have been more successful." She sighed.

"Stop it. You are successful. You're one of the best bakers in the state, and you're a terrific mother."

She smiled. "Thanks. Anyhow, that's neither here nor there. Now, try to think about the carjacking from those guys' point of view. You don't have a vehicle that runs. You're wanted for armed robbery and possibly murder. You need another car right away. So, what to do? You hijack the first person who comes along, and that just happened to be you. Let's face it, Sal. You're a main attraction for criminals. They all seem to know right where to find you."

"You're doing wonders for my self-confidence. What do you think happened to the money they got from the robberies?"

"My guess is that they were involved in a drug ring with

Damian. There must be a ringleader they're reporting back to—someone who's handling all the dough. The two that accosted you sound like a couple of morons."

I mulled this over for a minute. It wasn't a bad theory. "Maybe the Jolly-less Santas are here at the mall. They might be trying to blend in with the other ones."

"That wouldn't surprise me, but I'm guessing that Brian—or Brian's coworkers—have already checked out the ones who work here," Josie said. "Why don't we plan to come back tomorrow after work, when we have more time to check them all out. How does that sound?"

"It's worth a shot." We rounded the corner, and the hair salon came into view on my right. I glanced inside the plateglass window and let out a shriek. A pretty blonde in her mid to late twenties was talking to a Santa Claus.

"Oh God," I whispered. "Could he be one of my assailants?"

Josie put an arm around me. "Sal, calm down. Like I said, this mall is full of Santas this time of year. You can't let every single one spook you."

How sad was it to be afraid of Santa Claus? With trepidation, I followed Josie, who held the salon door open for me. The blonde and Santa looked over at us. "Be with you in a sec," she said.

Santa put out his hand for the woman to shake and exited the shop. A thought occurred to me, but a second too late. The beard—was it cream colored? I hadn't gotten a good look at it. Damn! The baby kicked, and my abdomen tightened. I shut my eyes tight until the contraction passed.

"Sal?" Josie whispered in my ear. "Are you okay? Is it time?"

Dang, this kid was as stubborn as Mrs. Gavelli in search of a good fortune cookie message. "No, false alarm."

"Probably because you're stressed from seeing Mr. Ho Ho Ho," she said grimly.

The woman walked over to us. She was pretty in a delicate sort of way, her blonde hair cut in a pixie style and skin so pale it was transparent. Crystal clear blue eyes scanned us up and down. "Do you ladies have an appointment?"

"Are you Rachel by chance?"

She studied me. "That's right. But I don't have anyone scheduled for the rest of the night. Did someone recommend me?"

I glanced around the shop. There were three stations, with the one to the far left occupied by an elderly woman who had her head wrapped in foil. A woman who bore a striking resemblance to Elvira was adjusting said foil. Other than them, the shop appeared to be empty. "Do you have a couple of minutes to talk—about Damian Ruger?"

Rachel narrowed her eyes. "Who are you? Cops?"

I had a sudden urge to laugh. "No. We went to school with Damian." I didn't want to divulge my true identity. "A friend said you were dating him. We're very sorry for your loss."

She laughed bitterly and placed her hands on her full, rounded hips. "Right. Come on. I know who you really are. Sally Donovan, the one who dated him in high school. The one whose cake server was found next to his body. You hated him for dumping you and accused him of the carjacking to get even." Rachel thrust a finger in my face. "I read the article. I saw your picture in the paper."

So much for trying to keep anything a secret in this town. "Look. Think about how preposterous this sounds. Why would I be holding a grudge against Damian for 16 years? That's more than half of my life! I'm here because I want to clear my name."

"We know that Damian wasn't one of her carjackers," Josie said. "Who was the Santa that just left here?"

Rachel tossed her head. "That old guy? He works for the local mission. They've been good to me in the past when I needed help. He comes in every year for a donation. I don't make much, but always give something. We have to pay it forward, you know?"

"Do you own the salon?" Josie asked.

She shook her head. "No. Angie, the owner, will be back by closing, and she hates to see us standing around. If you plan on talking some more, you'd better get ready for a dye job." She studied Josie's beautiful auburn hair closely. "You could use one, honey. Looks like you're getting a few grays."

"Excuse me?" Josie exploded.

I didn't see any gray hairs on Josie's head, but knew that I had a few. Mine were probably the result of stress. Being a murder suspect might do it. The customer with the foil on her head was beaming in the mirror at her pink-colored strands. I shuddered and reached inside my purse for a twenty-dollar bill. "Ah, instead of giving Josie a dye job, maybe this will help."

Rachel's eyes widened at the bill. She glanced around and then snatched it from my outstretched hand. "Okay, look. I don't know who really killed Damian, but I can assure you it wasn't me. I went to his apartment to meet someone."

Josie frowned. "Meet who? Were you getting back together with Damian?"

She shook her head vehemently. "No way. I was supposed to meet Farley there, but he got hung up at work."

The name struck a familiar chord with me. "Who's Farley?"

"Damian's best friend and my boyfriend. They've known each other for years."

"Farley Drake? He was ahead of us in school by a couple of years," Josie mused. "I didn't know him personally though."

Rachel beamed. "The one and only. He's a great guy. Farley doesn't force me to take drugs like Damian did or knock me around."

"That must make him the perfect boyfriend," Josie said dryly.

She frowned. "I don't appreciate sarcasm, honey. You can laugh if you want, but he's ten times the man Damian was. That creep was always smacking me around. Then he'd call up the next day and lay on the charm, begging me to come back to him. I ended up in rehab thanks to him, but I'm clean now. There's no way in hell I'd ever go back to him."

The entire scenario didn't make any sense. "Why would you even step foot in Damian's apartment when he used to treat you like dirt?"

Josie folded her arms across her chest. "And why would Farley still hang out with a dirtbag who did such awful things to his girlfriend?"

Rachel glared at us both. "You don't understand. He's

changed. I had no interest in Damian romantically, even though he wasn't doing drugs anymore. He was a kinder, gentler man."

Josie snorted back a laugh, which she immediately turned into a cough. I wasn't buying this bull of Rachel's either. I was sorry Damian had died, but it was hard for me to believe he'd done a complete turnaround.

"What happened when you got to Damian's apartment that night?" I asked.

She sat down in one of the station chairs and clasped her hands in her lap. "I saw the cop cars out front, but that didn't bother me. There's always some loser getting in trouble over there. So, I went up the back stairway to Damian's pad. When I got near his apartment, the cops told me I needed to leave. They wouldn't tell me what was going on either. And then I saw *her*."

"You saw *who*?" Terror seeped into my bones, and for a brief second, I was afraid she might indicate me. 'Tis the season for paranoia.

"Magnolia." She spat the name out as if it were venom. "That cheap tramp was standing by the door of the apartment, sobbing on some good-looking cop's shoulder. What a freaking phony. It wouldn't surprise me if she killed Damian."

CHAPTER NINE

Josie and I exchanged glances. "Why would Magnolia want to kill Damian?" I asked.

Rachel shot me a funny look. "Because she thought he was seeing someone behind her back—namely, yours truly. She's always been jealous of me."

I shook my head, hoping the action might settle the pieces of this puzzle in my brain. "Okay. Let me get this straight. You dated Damian. Now you're dating his friend Farley. Magnolia was back to dating Damian, but in turn she thought he was dating someone behind her back—you. Am I missing anything?"

She studied her French manicure and then pinned me with a direct gaze. "The article said that your cake server was found next to his body. It seems crazy that you'd kill him because he dumped you back in high school, but I have a friend who did something similar. She's up for parole in 20 years."

I sucked in some air. Forget the cake server as a weapon. When I found Jerry Maroon, I might choke him to death. "What else do you know?" A picture of Josie's gingerbread cookies with the strawberry icing entered my mind. "Was anything else found at the crime scene?"

Rachel shrugged. "I'm not sure. They wouldn't let me in the apartment, so I couldn't see what was going on. When I got back to my car, a body was brought out on a gurney, and I knew it had to be Damian's."

"But you couldn't be sure that it was *his* body," Josie pointed out. "What if Damian had killed someone in his apartment and left the body there?"

Rachel glanced slyly at me. "Damian told Farley that

you still had the hots for him after all these years. It's the first thing Farley mentioned when I saw him earlier today."

These people were all nuts. I knew that drugs could affect one's brain, but did it also render them completely senseless? How could they possibly believe such a dumb story? A tremor of fear shot through me. Both these women had a motive to kill Damian, so what would stop them from lying about seeing me at his apartment that night? It would only be my word against theirs. "Any idea who else might want Damian dead?"

She gave me the evil eye. "I just told you that it was Magnolia—unless you really did do it."

Josie held up a hand. "Okay, let's play a game. Pretend for a minute that neither Magnolia nor Sal killed Damian. Is there anyone else who wouldn't mind putting Damian six feet under?"

Her tone was patronizing and made me wince. I loved Josie dearly, but she was not always the most subtle person when it came to interrogation tactics.

Rachel wrinkled her tiny nose, the diamond embedded on one side winking in the bright light from above. "Yeah, I guess. He had his share of enemies. Damian may have owed people money for drugs, although he's been clean for a while. Maybe Farley would know."

"Where can I find him?" I asked.

"Give me your phone number, and I'll ask him to call you. No guarantees though. He's a very busy and important guy."

The mystery man had me intrigued. "What does Farley do for a living?"

Rachel puffed out her chest with an air of importance. "He works at Colwestern's Car Wash. He's the manager." She tossed her head proudly. "I get free car washes."

"Lucky you," Josie muttered. "All the fringe benefits."

Rachel glared at her. "What's that supposed to mean?"

I gave Josie a slight nudge in the side. "Uh, is there a chance that Farley—" *Walk softly, Sal.* "Was he involved in Damian's line of work too?"

She shot me a look of utter disbelief. "Of course not. I mean, maybe a little recreational use every now and then. Heck, we all do it, right? But Damian—when we dated—he'd get angry after he used. He once hit a cop and landed in the slammer for a couple of months. And then one time he got pulled over for speeding, and the cops found a stash in his car. Damian was a good-looking dude, but not very bright. There was a time when he'd do anything to get drugs—even kill for them. That's what addiction can do to a person."

Josie and I exchanged glances. "He killed someone?" I asked.

Rachel shook her head. "Nah. He was a murder suspect last summer, but the cops cleared him. Funny how he cleaned up his act right after that—or said he did. Guess he finally learned his lesson."

Now she had my attention. "Really? What happened?"

Rachel glanced out into the mall's concourse and gave a sudden start. "Uh-oh. That's my boss. If you're not getting your hair done, you need to leave."

I handed Rachel one of my business cards right before a woman with spiked, purple hair entered the salon. "Please have Farley call me. And if you think of anything else that might help, would you get in touch?"

She eyed me sharply and nodded. "Hell, if you're handing out twenties, I'll tell you anything you want to know."

When we exited the shop and stepped into the main concourse, I almost ran right into another Santa. He grinned and tipped his hat at me. "Merry Christmas, little lady." He stared down at my protruding belly and grinned. "And company."

"Good grief." I blew out a breath. "They're everywhere."

"What'd I tell you? That's why I don't like to bring the kids here," Josie remarked. "It's too confusing. Are we done for tonight? I have to get home soon so that Rob can leave for work."

We were near the front entrance. "Yes, I'm tired anyway." And depressed, but didn't add that part.

"Oh crap," Josie said as we got into the van. "I must have left my wallet at the bakery. Do you mind if we stop there first so that I can grab it?"

"Of course not." Wearily, I closed my eyes and settled back against the headrest. The walking had done a number on me, and I was ready for dreamland.

Josie started the engine. "I can come pick you up after work tomorrow if you feel like doing some more sleuthing. That is," she said with a grin, "if Baby Donovan doesn't make an appearance by then."

I wondered how many women had babies in prison cells. Maybe I'd google it when I got home. "I don't have much choice. We could plan for five o'clock and catch Santa before he leaves for the night." I opened my eyes and stared out the window at the lighted candy canes displayed on a front lawn we were passing. The next house had a giant Frosty the Snowman waving from its rooftop. Christmas was almost here, my favorite time of year. The season for perpetual hope, which I needed desperately right now. "If someone accuses me, I'm done for. You might as well get out the orange jumpsuit."

Josie opened her mouth to say something, but the buzzing of my phone cut her off. I glanced down at the screen. The number was local and familiar, but I couldn't place it. "Hello?"

"Sally, it's Adam. Adam Greensburg—Brian's partner."

My mouth went dry. Why was he calling me? Whatever the reason, it couldn't be good. "Uh, hi. What's up?"

"I wanted to give you an update on what's going on," he said. "Brian asked me to phone you. We think the Jolly-less Santas are still in town. In fact, the convenience store over on Broadway was hit about two hours ago. The surveillance camera caught two Santas driving away in a beat-up Ford."

I clutched the phone tightly behind my hands. "I don't understand. How do these guys keep getting away with this?"

"They probably have someone helping them behind the scenes," Adam said. "Maybe a former employee who knows the layouts of these stores. Don't worry. We'll catch them. By the way, Brian asked me to deliver a message to you."

Oh joy. "Gee let me guess. He said for me to stay out of it and to let the police handle everything."

Adam chuckled into the phone. "I guess you do know him pretty well." He paused for a moment. "Look, I know how terrifying this must be for you, especially in your condition, but you have to trust us. We're trained to find criminals like these.

One way or another, we'll get them." He clicked off without another word.

The phrase "one way or another" bothered me. Did that mean they'd catch these guys, but not before I was locked up behind iron bars?

Josie glanced sideways at me. "What's up?"

I relayed what Adam had said. "It sounds like going to the mall tomorrow could be a smart move on our part."

"Is there anything else you remember about the Santas?" Josie asked. "Ear piercings? Cologne smell? Bad breath?"

The breath mention triggered my memory. "One of them smelled like peppermints. I know it's not much to go on. Oh, and remember, I told you about the cream-colored beard. I wish I could think of something else."

She patted my hand. "You're probably trying to shut it all out because you were so scared. We'll find those bozos, don't you…" Her voice trailed off as she pulled into the alley behind the bakery. My father's car was parked in her usual spot. "Uh, Sal, why is your father here? At six o'clock on a Friday night?"

"Who knows?" I unbuckled my seat belt. "Maybe he needed a fortune cookie fix."

Josie frowned. "Did you give him the alarm code? There's no way I'd forget to set—"

"Yes," I interrupted. "Dad's had it since he had his book signing here. But it's not like him to stop in without telling me first." Oh no. That's when I remembered about the blogging class.

Josie swore softly under her breath as she unlocked the door to the kitchen. "What's he doing? Having another signing without telling us? Nothing about that man surprises me anymore."

This would. "He's teaching a class on blogging for the local college in the apartment upstairs."

She looked at me in amazement. "You're joking!"

"Don't I wish. But I thought he was planning to hold the classes on Saturday mornings. At least that's what he told me. Maybe they're baking fortune cookies." I tried to laugh it off, but Josie was having none of it. *Please, please, don't let him do anything crazy.* "I'm sure everything is fine."

She snorted as we made our way to the staircase. "Right. Your father doesn't cause problems. That's like saying it will never snow in Buffalo again."

Muffled voices could be heard from the upstairs apartment. *Oh boy.* "Here goes nothing." We started up the stairs. I was slow and breathing heavily before we even made it up halfway. I almost expected my water to break from the exertion.

Josie brought up the rear. "Take your time. I'll catch you if you fall."

What a cheerful thought. "If this doesn't put me into labor, nothing will," I panted.

We peered into the open doorway of the apartment. Although currently vacant, it had seen its share of action in the past two years since we'd reopened at this location. Gianna had rented the apartment for a while, and then a friend of Nicoletta's ran a business here briefly before meeting her untimely demise. My father had used the space for a book signing that I was certain was unlike any other author's. The combination living and dining room were now filled with three rows of desks and chairs. All were occupied.

"Hello?" I said, trying to catch my breath. Nine heads looked up from their laptops.

"Hi, baby girl!" My father came over to greet us. "I know you weren't expecting me here so soon, but I thought I'd do an introductory class tonight since everyone was available. I didn't think you'd mind, because it was after hours."

"Domenic, you're certainly full of surprises," Josie remarked.

My father puffed out his chest in an exaggerated manner and spread his arms out wide. "Class, I'd like you to meet my daughter Sally Donovan and her head baker, Josie Sullivan. Sal's the big round one. As you can see, my grandchild is late arriving. But as we all know, Italian babies come whenever they darn well feel like it."

I struggled not to roll my eyes. "Dad, you've got such a way with words. Remember, this baby is also part Irish."

He waved a hand dismissively. "Ah, the Italian side always dominates."

With unabashed curiosity, I glanced around at Dad's "students." I wondered where he'd had the desks delivered from. They looked brand new. Maybe they'd been sitting in the basement of a friend's funeral parlor. Maybe he'd be teaching a class on embalming next. One never knew with my father.

Each student had a laptop and a copy of my father's book, *How to Plan and Enjoy Your Funeral*, on top of their desk. My father was using the dining room table Gianna had left behind as his work desk at the front of the room. A chalkboard on wheels stood next to it. He'd written on the board in large block letters, *The Art of Death Blogging*.

Kill me now.

My father's students varied considerably in age, with at least sixty years between them. The youngest student looked like he might still be in high school, while the oldest could have been my father's dad. That particular student was none other than Nicoletta's main squeeze, Ronald Feathers. He was hard of hearing, which wasn't necessarily a bad thing where Nicoletta was concerned.

He peered at me through his bifocals and winked. "Hi ya, cutie. Haven't popped yet, huh?"

My father rubbed his hands together in satisfaction. "Yep, that's me. Always full of surprises. Hey, you girls are just in time to see what everyone is working on." He rapped his ruler on the table. "How about it, gang? Mind if Sally takes a peek at your blogs?"

"Dad, that's not necessary," I demurred, not wanting to see what they were writing about. Most likely it concerned death, funerals, or any other morbid topic my father could think of.

A woman of about fifty crooked her finger at me. "Come and see mine, hon. It's all about how I plan to become a mortuary makeup artist. I'm licensed in cosmetology, and I sell Mary Kay, so I'm already way ahead of the game." She handed me and Josie each a Mary Kay catalog. "My number is on the back if you want to order anything. Ten percent off for Dom's family and friends. We're running a great special on cover-up this month."

"I'll keep it in mind," I said.

High heels clacked against the wooden stairs, and my mother appeared in the doorway, dressed in a one-shoulder, shiny silver mesh dress that barely covered her rear. How she never caught pneumonia dressed like that in the winter always mystified me.

"Hello, darling. Hi, Josie. What a nice surprise." She came over to kiss me on the cheek then pranced to the front of the room, handing my father a cup of coffee. "I'm the classroom monitor," she said proudly.

"You can monitor me anytime, honey," Mr. Feathers called out.

My mother trotted back over to me and patted my belly. "How's my grandbaby doing today? Ready to come out?"

"I think that kid's glued in there," my father commented before clapping his hands. "Okay, now everyone else besides Thelma, go ahead and tell the girls about your blogs."

I glanced sideways at Josie, and she nodded. We started to move toward the doorway. One step at a time—

The high school kid waved a hand at us. "Come on over. I'm Freddie Price. My blog isn't about death. Not directly, anyway."

"He's such a breath of fresh air, isn't he?" My mother giggled as Josie and I approached Freddie's desk.

"He still qualifies for the class," my father explained, as if I was worried about it. "His blog is more like the TV show *Cold Justice*. I tell you, this kid is going places."

"Are you the odd man out?" Josie asked him. "Or the dead man out?"

Josie and I both laughed at her pun. When we noticed we were the only two doing so, we quickly stopped. Talk about your awkward moments.

Freddie smiled politely at us. He was an attractive guy with dark wavy hair and clear gray eyes. "I'm in my last year at SUNY Buffalo."

He was older than I'd thought. "That's a good college."

He flushed with pride. "I'm doing an internship at the *Colwestern Journal*. My blog focuses on unsolved deaths in Colwestern and the surrounding areas." He stared at me with new interest. "I've read about the murder cases you've solved. You're like a legend around here. Maybe I could interview you sometime for the blog."

"Ah, I don't know." What I really meant to say was, *Over* my *dead body.*

"She'd be glad to help," my father insisted while I shot him a death glare.

Freddie prattled on, oblivious to the daggers I was shooting my father. "I really want to be a reporter. My friend Jerry mentioned you in his column recently. He's such an inspiration to me."

I sucked in a breath. "Jerry Maroon is your *friend*?" The name incensed me more every time I heard it.

"He's a great guy," Freddie insisted. "Jerry knows exactly what he's doing."

Josie snorted. "Oh, he sure does." She leaned over Freddie's shoulder for a closer look at the computer screen. "What's this particular case about?"

Freddie smiled, his perfect white teeth gleaming as he pointed at the screen. "This one happened last summer. It wasn't in Colwestern though. I've always been fascinated by cold cases." He looked at me hopefully. "Have you ever solved one?"

I racked my brain, trying to remember. "Once. An elderly woman who was poisoned at an assisted living home several years ago."

Freddie snapped his fingers. "Oh yeah, I remember that one. Wow, you're good." The respect was evident in his tone. "I really hope you didn't kill that Damian fellow like Jerry said. It would totally ruin your sleuthing career."

I gritted my teeth together. "Not to worry. It wasn't me."

Josie was silently reading Freddie's page as we talked. "A woman fell over the side of a steamboat last summer, but you don't believe it was an accident? I think I remember reading about that in the paper when it happened."

He nodded eagerly. "Her name was Tatiana Richards. The cops said that she was so high on drugs that she must have fallen over the side. Someone spotted her in the water right away, and they managed to get her out, but it was too late. Guess she hit her head when she went over the side, and the medical examiner said the blow could have contributed to her death. Jerry thinks there's more to it than what the cops said. He thinks someone pushed her."

Josie kept reading. "It says that she was a crackhead and had been busted for drugs a few times." She pursed her lips together. "Maybe she was so out of it that she thought she could fly off the boat. I've heard of things like that happening."

Freddie shook his head. "Jerry says she was pushed. He was an anchorman for Channel 11 news at the time and was one of the first people on the scene."

"Funny how he always seems to do that," Josie remarked.

Freddie stared at her in confusion but went on. "Jerry said he saw part of a footprint near the railing, and judging by the size, it couldn't be hers. But it got washed away before he could tell anyone."

"Did he report it to the police?" I asked.

"Of course," Freddie said. "Jerry's such a stand-up guy."

"Okay, I just threw up a little in my mouth," Josie whispered.

My father came over and proudly patted Freddie on the shoulder. "Isn't he great? A student like this—they make it all worth it, Sal."

"Sure, Dad." I was tempted to ask what "it" was, but decided I was better off not knowing.

CHAPTER TEN

"Don't forget to breathe, princess."

I stopped huffing and puffing long enough to stare into Mike's handsome face. He was grinning from ear to ear as he stood at my bedside, holding my hand. "It will all be over soon," he said.

I smiled up at him. "In a few minutes, we're going to see our sweet baby. I can't believe the time's finally come." The urge to push was great, and I tried to concentrate on Mike's face. This wasn't so bad. The labor pains didn't hurt nearly as bad as everyone had said.

"Come on, baby girl," my father's voice urged. "You're almost there."

My head whipped to the right, and I blinked once, no, twice. The delivery room was filled to capacity with members of my family. *What the—*

My father stood a few feet away from the bed and in full view of the labor process, to my horror. He munched away on one of Josie's jelly cookies while my mother peered over his shoulder with a video camera.

"We can see the head!" she announced excitedly. "I'll bet it's a boy! Jerry Maroon said he'll try to fit part of my actual delivery footage on the news tonight."

"He *what*?" I screeched and then looked back at my husband. "What's going on? Are we selling tickets?"

Gianna stood next to the doctor with Alex in her arms, feeding him a bottle. "Go, Sal, go! You're doing great! Can you move a little faster though? You need to be dressed for my wedding in an hour."

Johnny appeared behind Gianna and gave me a thumbs-up. "You're not even screaming or smacking Mike around like Gianna did to me. Nice job, Sal!"

Gianna's face turned beet red as she glared at her fiancé. "If you think it's so easy to give birth, feel free to try!"

Mrs. Gavelli pushed her way in between my parents for a look, then clucked her tongue at me. She held a fortune cookie in one hand and a handmade black baby blanket in the other. She tried to hand it to the doctor, whose head was bent over in concentration. "You put baby on this. It wards bad spirits away. Ancient Italian secret. Yo, missy." She shook her finger at me. "You bring more fortune cookies?"

"Mike?" My voice quavered as I turned to my husband, but he was on his cell. He smiled at me and squeezed my hand. "Sal, you're going to have to move a little faster. The Fosters have a leaky roof."

"It's a boy, Sally!" the doctor announced as everyone clapped and cheered. "And he's absolutely perfect."

The doctor's voice sounded familiar—*too* familiar. My mouth went dry as he raised his head over the sheet to look up at me, and I gasped. Brian removed his surgical mask and grinned, then held up a pair of shiny silver handcuffs. "Oh, and by the way, you're under arrest."

I screamed.

The light flicked on, and Mike leaned over me in our bed, his blue eyes anxious. "Sal, what's wrong? Is it time to go?"

Relief swept over me. It had all been a dream—*no,* an actual nightmare. Exhausted, I ran a hand across my damp forehead. "Oh God. I just had the worst dream."

Mike's strong arms went around my shoulders as he cradled me against his bare rock-hard chest. "Shh. It's all going to be fine. I'm sure all expectant mothers go through this." He chuckled. "Maybe you shouldn't have eaten tacos and pickles for dinner tonight."

I stared up at him and burst into tears.

His expression was horrified. "Oh, sweetheart, I was only kidding. You can eat anything you want. You're not fat—hell, that's only baby fat. Get it? You look beautiful and—"

"It's not that," I wept. "I'm so scared."

"About the delivery?" He kissed my hair. "There's no

need to worry. I'll be with you every step of the way."

"No. I mean, I'm a little scared about the pain, but—" I sat up straighter and leaned my back against the headboard. "I'm afraid that I'll have my baby in prison. Or they'll take me away in handcuffs right after I have him—or her." My hands rested on top of my belly. "I've wanted this for so long, and now I'm terrified that something bad is going to happen."

Mike stroked my hair gently. "You're not going to jail, Sal. I'll never let that happen. Over my dead body."

"But *someone* wants me to go to jail for this. Why me? If it weren't for that blasted Jerry Maroon, I might have been able to narrow down who did this by now. Thanks to him, everyone knows my cake server was the murder weapon." A lightbulb went on in my head. "Wait a second. No one knows about the gingerbread cookies next to Damian's body, except for the police, Josie, and me."

"What difference does that make?" Mike asked.

"Maybe that would help us to figure out who the real killer is," I said thoughtfully. "Rachel, his ex, didn't know, but Damian's girlfriend, Magnolia, must have seen the cookies because she found him." She also knew about the cake server. Could she know something else she hadn't told the police? "If I can meet with her and—"

"No." Mike's tone was sharp. "It's far too dangerous, Sal. I'm putting my foot down this time. I won't have you playing detective in your condition."

Tears ran down my cheeks. "What other choice do I have? Brian's removed himself from the case. Why haven't the cops found the Jolly-less Santas yet? They may not be that smart, but they've managed to outwit everyone so far. Why haven't the security cameras caught them? Everyone has one these days."

"Stay calm, princess. Don't get yourself all worked up. It's not good for you or the baby."

I reached for his hand. "I'm not saying that I can do a better job than the police, but I have to try. Josie and I won't do anything dangerous, and I'd never put our baby in jeopardy. You know that. Please trust me, okay? We're only going shopping at the mall tomorrow, and if we spot any suspicious-looking Santas, we'll alert the police."

That got a smile out of him. "It's pretty sad when Santa starts looking suspicious." His voice became gruff. "It's going to happen, Sal. You, me, and our baby are going to have a wonderful Christmas together—the first of many." He placed his lips over mine, and desire swept over me like a tidal wave. At that moment, the baby gave a sharp kick, and Mike rubbed my stomach gently. "Seems like someone wants us to knock it off."

I laughed. "I wish he or she would hurry up and get here."

"It won't be long now. How about some hot chocolate?" Mike suggested. "It might help you sleep."

"No, thanks. I just want you to hold me."

"That can easily be arranged," he said softly.

I laid down on my back and adjusted the pillow between my legs. It seemed to help with the leg and back pain.

Mike draped his arm over my belly and lay on his side facing me. "See? And you were worried that I couldn't put my arms around you anymore," he chuckled.

"You take care of everything." We were quiet for a few minutes, and I listened to the wind howling outside, grateful for Mike, my family, and my precious little one. "This baby still needs a name."

"I'm working on it," Mike said. "But I think that I need to see her face first. Then inspiration will strike."

I yawned and snuggled closer to him. "So, you think we're having a girl?"

"I know we are." He kissed my hair and closed his eyes.

"Well, Mr. Donovan, I'm convinced that we're having a boy. And he's going to look just like his daddy. Mrs. Gavelli thinks it's a boy too. She said she received a fortune cookie message confirming it."

Mike snorted in my ear. "Mrs. Gavelli ought to mind her own business. Better yet, maybe she should pay more attention to the fortune cookies and leave your sister alone. Johnny told me yesterday that he's afraid Gianna's going to crack like one if the old lady doesn't back off."

"Josie always says that Mrs. Gavelli could scare Satan."

"Or Santa for that matter," Mike said sleepily.

My eyes flickered open in the semidarkness, and I

gasped. "Jeez, do you realize if you move the *n* and *t* in Satan, it spells Santa?"

"Enough, Sal." Mike yawned. "You need to stop looking at every Santa like they're a potential killer. I want our child to believe in him for as long as possible."

This surprised me. "I had no idea you felt that way."

"Sure I do." He opened his eyes. "It's good for kids to have something to believe in—especially those who don't have much else to look forward to."

A lump formed in my throat. He was talking about his own childhood. Unlike mine, it had not been a happy one.

To my amazement, Mike chuckled. "Did I ever tell you about the one time I went to see Santa?"

"No, but I want to hear all about it." Mike rarely talked about his childhood, and I knew why—the memories were too painful. His mother had been drunk most of the time, his dad had deserted him at the age of five, and his stepfather was an abusive, cruel man. I'd never thought about this before, but it made sense that he would believe in Santa. Hope and faith were important to everyone, but especially a child.

His voice was soft against my ear. "It was right after my father had left. Mom was trying to sober up, but that didn't last long. I kept asking for a new bike, and she told me we couldn't afford one. So I begged her to take me to see Santa. I knew he'd bring me one if only I could go see him in person. Mom felt bad about Dad leaving, so she agreed."

Mike propped himself up on one elbow and was staring down into my face, but I could tell that his mind was somewhere else. Back to another time and place, over 25 years ago. I reached up to stroke his hair. "Go on."

He cleared his throat. "I didn't tell my mother that there was something else I wanted to ask Santa for, because she never would have taken me then."

I had a hunch what it was but remained silent.

Mike pursed his lips. "When it was finally my turn to sit on his lap, I asked him if he would bring my father back."

Tears stung the corners of my eyes. "What did he say?"

Mike wove his fingers through my hair. "Santa told me he didn't have the power to do things like that. I said, okay, if my father couldn't come back, then I'd take the bike." His midnight blue eyes twinkled at me. "I was quite the negotiator from a young age."

"I can see that about you. Then what happened?"

Mike stared thoughtfully at me, with an innocent look of wonder that made him seem much younger than his thirty-one years. "On Christmas morning, there it was, standing next to the tree. A Huffy yellow and blue bike. Training wheels and all." He smiled tenderly at me. "Year later I found out that my mother had sold her wedding ring to get me the bike. She may not have been mother of the year, but she did want me to have a good Christmas—the first one without my father there."

"Oh my." Hot, fat tears trickled down my face like a fountain. "That's a beautiful story."

He swiped under my eyes with the pad of his thumb. "It's a magical season, especially for kids, Sal." His voice had turned gruff. "And I want our child to enjoy every minute of it, every year."

The tears showed no sign of letting up as I placed my arms around his neck, and he held me tightly against him. We lay there holding each other close and saying nothing for several minutes. When Mike finally drew back to kiss me, I noticed that his face was damp too.

CHAPTER ELEVEN

The day stretched out before me like an endless road in the desert. I had nothing to do except wait and see what happened first—my baby arrived, or I wound up in jail.

Mike planned to finish up a couple of odd jobs today, and then he was done with work until I had the baby. The house had been decorated and my shopping and wrapping long since completed. For once, my house was clean, and the baby's room all ready for him or her. I'd folded and refolded all the baby onesies, nightgowns, and receiving blankets at least three times in as many days. Being in the baby's room helped with my anxiety, and I enjoyed sitting in the rocker every night, looking at the *Goodnight Moon* and *Pat the Bunny* books I couldn't wait to read to my child.

With a sigh, I went to the kitchen for my morning cup of hated decaf. Spike lay curled in his bed by the stove, sound asleep. When I spoke his name, he opened one eye, looked at me, and then shut it again, snoring even louder. He was as bored with me as I was with my current situation.

This was ridiculous. I felt fine, and there was no reason why I couldn't drive to the bakery and try to help Josie with last-minute Christmas baking. Plus, I had to find a way to clear my name from Damian's murder. Maybe we could leave Dodie in charge for an hour or two this afternoon. It was risky to leave her there, but I couldn't go without Josie.

When I arrived at the shop, I was dismayed to see that there was only one customer in the shop. There should have been a line of people out the door. Apparently, everyone in Colwestern thought a nine-month pregnant woman was still capable of murder.

"What are you doing here?" Josie asked me in amazement as she handed a pink box to Mrs. O'Brien.

I gave her my best Cheshire cat grin. "Sorry, but don't I still own this place?"

Mrs. O'Brien brought a hand to her mouth. "Goodness! Sally Donovan, you haven't had that baby yet? Look how big you are…are you sure it's not twins?"

"Nope. There's only one baby in there. Guess he's going to be a big one, huh?" I winked at Josie as Mrs. O'Brien came over and put her hand on my stomach. It annoyed me when people other than my family or Josie did this. Mrs. O'Brien was one of our best customers, so I suppressed an urge to smack her hand way.

Mrs. O'Brien frowned, the age spots on her cheeks growing larger. "Oh, my dear. I was smaller than you and in labor with my Jake for two whole days. I hope that doesn't happen to you."

Her tone sounded gleeful, almost as if she did hope it would happen. I bit into my lower lip, trying to keep a sarcastic comment escaping.

Josie came to stand next to me. "Sal, I need your opinion on something in the back room. Have a nice day, Mrs. O'Brien."

"Not so fast, honey," Mrs. O'Brien huffed. "You didn't give me my fortune cookie yet."

"Oh, I'll give you a cookie," Josie mumbled under her breath. She started toward the display case, when her cell phone rang.

I held up a hand. "Go ahead and answer that. It could be an order. I'll get her cookie. I'm still allowed to lift one of those, right?"

"Listen to that sarcastic mouth of yours. Who do you think you are—me?" Josie winked and went into the back room.

I grabbed a piece of waxed paper from the box on the counter and reached into the case to grab a fortune cookie, which was stuck to another one. When I pulled them apart, the message in one popped out and stared me in the face.

You'd better watch out, you better not cry…

Good grief. I slammed the case shut with a bang and thrust the still intact cookie at Mrs. O'Brien, who stared back at me wide-eyed. The expression on my face must not have been jolly, because she exited the shop without another word. Josie came back into the room as I dumped the other cookie into the trash.

"Should I even ask?"

"No. Let's not go there," I said.

She walked into the kitchen, and I followed. "You shouldn't be here," Josie said as she reached for a tray of macarons. "If you go into labor, Mike's going to yell at me."

"Don't be ridiculous," I scoffed and nodded at Dodie, who was decorating a tray of gingerbread men. "Don't you need help finishing the order for the bank's Christmas party? It's tonight, right?"

Josie sprinkled almonds on a tray of lemon macaroons that were ready to go into the oven. "Dodie's working on the gingerbread. I only need to do the rest of the tree cookies and some chocolate-filled cookie cups."

My mouth watered at the mention of them. We'd recently added the cookie cups to our menu, and they were a huge hit. They consisted of a chocolate chip cookie crust filled with rich melted chocolate in the middle, and it was impossible to eat just one.

Josie cocked her head at me. "Aren't the quarterly taxes due soon?"

Shoot. I'd almost forgotten. "Yes. I can work on those while I wait for you and finish them at home if necessary. Once everything is in order—" I glanced over at Dodie, absorbed in decorating the cookies. "Perhaps we can take off for a bit?"

Josie nodded. "Yes. Mickey's on his way in. I was going to tell him to forget about coming since it's been so slow, but it won't hurt to have him here, *if* you know what I mean."

The row of silver bells on the front door jingled, and Josie held up a hand. "I've got it."

I grabbed the paperwork from the safe I kept near the walk-in freezer. Dodie was still in her own little world, humming to herself as she placed raisins on a gingerbread man for his eyes and belly button. "How's everything going, Dodie?"

The elderly woman didn't answer. I moved closer and then noticed she was wearing earbuds. I caught the faint strands of "Santa Claus Is Coming to Town" and cringed inwardly.

"Dodie?" I called louder. Her head bobbed in time to the music, so I touched her gently on the arm.

Dodie's right arm jerked out, and she squirted icing down the front of my red V-neck T-shirt. "Oh no!" Dodie screamed. "Sally, I'm so sorry!"

"It's okay," I assured her and hastily went to the sink. I grabbed a sponge and worked at the stain, but my shirt was a mess. At least she'd missed hitting my coat, since I hadn't been able to button it for weeks.

Dodie wrung her hands in obvious distress. "I'm so sorry. I'll buy you a new shirt. What size are you wearing—"

She flung out her left hand, which connected with the bowl of icing. We both watched as the metal bowl flew into the air, flipped, and landed upside down on the floor, but not before it had flung icing everywhere—the stove top, metal cookie racks, and the front of the dishwasher. Dodie and I both bent down to pick up the bowl, and our heads collided. The impact caused me to stagger, and I landed hard on my backside.

Josie hurried in and gasped when she saw me sitting on the floor. "What the hell happened? Are you all right?"

"I think so. It was just a little accident." I accepted the hand she held out to me, and after a minute I was back on my feet.

Josie narrowed her eyes at Dodie. "Oh, I think I can guess what happened."

Dodie was in tears. "Oh, girls, I'm so sorry. Sally, I hope the baby is all right. I don't know what's the matter with me. I've never been so clumsy."

"Only since birth," Josie said between gritted teeth and then turned to me. "If you're okay, someone's here to see you. That friend of Damian's."

There was a Sally's Samples sweatshirt hanging on one of the brass wall hooks. The size read extra-extra-large. My father had asked for it but then ended up needing a smaller size. I slipped the shirt over my stained one, and it fit perfectly. It bothered me a bit to realize that I was now a larger size than my father, but I assured my deflated ego that it was only temporary. "Who's here to see me? Farley Drake?"

Josie nodded. "I don't trust anyone who was friends with Damian. Don't worry—I'm not going to leave you alone with him for one single minute." She put an arm around me and looked over her shoulder at Dodie. "Mickey will be in to help you shortly. After we talk to the man out front, Sally and I are taking off for a spell."

Dodie looked up from sweeping the floor to smile at us and almost sent the broom into a tray of gingerbread cookies. She smiled encouragingly. "You two go ahead. I'll take good care of everything here."

"Sure she will," Josie whispered as we went into the storefront. "I may have to shoot her before the day is over just to get peace."

When I laid eyes on Farley Drake, memories crowded my brain. Farley had been two years ahead of us in high school and, like Damian, always surrounded by girls. He was another one with that bad-boy image I'd always found appealing. Mike once had that quality too, but in a different way. At least he'd had the sense to stay away from drugs and alcohol in high school. Instead, his parents had been the ones with addiction problems.

An evil-looking grin spread across Farley's face as he watched us approach, and his eyes lingered a bit too long on Josie's slender figure. I studied him for a minute, trying to remember what the appeal had been. Whatever it was had disappeared long ago with Farley's former toffee-colored hair, which was now bleached blond. His matching bushy eyebrows had a ring piercing through each one, and he wore a diamond stud in his left ear.

"Hello, Farley," I said.

"Yeah, I remember you and Red here." His mouth twitched under the full beard, also bleached blond. He probably spent more time on his appearance than I did. "Damian said you were still hung up on him, but I gotta say, you don't look like no killer to me. Guess I'm in the minority though."

A knot formed in the pit of my stomach. Why was everyone so obsessed with what had happened sixteen years ago? "Rachel must have given you my message."

Deep-set gray eyes fixated on me. "Why were you bothering my girl?"

"Hold on a second," Josie interrupted. "We weren't bothering anyone. Sal's trying to find out who killed your friend and clear herself from the suspect list."

Farley's gaze traveled down to my stomach. "I don't know why everyone's making such a fuss, even if it was your cake server that killed him. It would be hard for you to kill somebody, being handicapped like that."

I struggled to keep my voice on an even keel. "Are you saying that having a baby handicaps a woman?"

He held up a hand in protest. "Whoa. That's not what I meant, little mama."

"Don't talk to her that way," Josie said sharply.

"Look," Farley said. "All I meant is that it would be difficult for you to do the deed in your state…er, condition."

I was slightly less insulted. At least this guy wasn't accusing me of murder—yet. "Would you like to sit down?" I gestured at one of the tables by the bay window.

Farley plopped down in a chair and stretched his long legs under the table. He stared with interest at the display case while I watched. Was he a user too? He didn't have any visible signs, but if he and Damian had been friends for a long time, it was possible. "Would you like coffee? Or a cookie?"

He licked his lips. "Yeah. Need something sweet." He watched with interest as Dodie came out of the back room with a tray of gingerbread for the case. I braced myself, waiting for her to slide into the wall with them. Josie rushed over to relieve her of the tray.

"I'll take two of those gingerbread dudes," Farley said.

"Josie, bring two of those cookies over for Farley, please," I called out.

She brought a paper plate with the cookies and set them down in front of him. Farley stared at them for several seconds, as if unsure what to do with them. "They won't bite." I laughed.

"Oh. Right." He gingerly broke the head off a gingerbread and popped it into his mouth.

"You knew about my carjacking?" I asked.

Farley chewed with all the subtleness of an alligator. "Yeah, Damian told me. He came by my place after he got back from the police station. He also said that Donovan had knocked you up."

I sucked in a sharp breath. "The correct term is *expecting* or *pregnant*. And Mike is my husband, not a casual date."

He shrugged. "Whatever."

Farley was making it difficult to be nice to him, but I didn't want to alienate the man yet. "Have the police talked to you about Damian's death?"

He nodded. "Yeah, but I don't know nothin'. I saw Damian when I was on my way to work. Rachel called me later to tell me what happened to him." He shook his head ruefully. "Damian had some issues, but he didn't deserve to go like that. Pretty brutal if you ask me."

"Rachel said you're the manager at the local car wash," Josie interrupted. "Do you wash the cars too?"

Farley chewed with his mouth wide open. "If someone doesn't show up for work, I gotta pitch in. Two guys called out sick that night."

Josie frowned with disgust as he continued to munch away. "Damn. Didn't your mother ever teach you any manners?"

I frowned, afraid she'd offended him, but Farley merely laughed. "Yeah. Rachel says I'm a regular cow when I eat. My family didn't have much when I was a kid. There were six of us in two rooms, and at dinnertime it was always a race to see who could get to eat the fastest." He chuckled, as if remembering. "Move it or lose it."

His comment made me ashamed of my earlier assumptions. Who was I to judge this man? Sure, he was friends with Damian, but that didn't necessarily make him a killer. I shifted the conversation back to the night Damian had died. "And you had to stay because the other guys didn't show?"

"That's right. I didn't get out of there until after seven. We were busy that night and being shorthanded put me behind. I had to drop the night deposit at the bank too."

That would put him at the car wash during Damian's death, which had occurred sometime between 6:00 and 6:30. I rested my elbows on the table. "It was twenty degrees on Saturday. People were still coming in to get their cars washed?"

Farley looked at me as if I'd been smoking something. "People come out in all kinds of weather to get their cars washed. Or they stop by to use the vacuums. A clean car makes for a happy owner."

Apparently, Farley had taken the company's motto to heart. "You were Damian's best friend. Who would have wanted him dead?"

Farley shoved the rest of the gingerbread into his mouth. "Let's face the facts, ladies. I loved Damian like a brother, but he didn't have a lot of fans. He was always looking for a way to score drugs and then get out of paying people for them."

I wrinkled my nose. "We heard that he'd been clean the last few months."

He shook his head sadly. "There're ways of getting around drug tests. He managed to fool his parole officer a couple of times."

Josie and I exchanged glances. "What about you?" she asked sharply. "Do you use too?"

Farley's eyes frosted over like an ice storm. "Look, honey. I won't deny I've done them before. But I was never a total cokehead like D was."

"Then why'd you hang out with him?" Josie snapped.

"Because I've known him since we were kids. We both came from broken homes and grew up with nothin'. You never turn your back on childhood friends, no matter what."

Josie's face colored slightly. She didn't respond, and I knew why—she could relate to what Farley was saying. Josie had come from a similar home with too many siblings to feed and not enough to always go around. Growing up, she'd eaten more dinners at my house than her own. Still, I was having a hard time swallowing the fact that Damian had been a devoted friend to Farley like Josie had always been to me.

"What about Magnolia?" I asked suddenly.

"What about her?" he snorted. "That chick is a tramp. She's hot and all, but still a tramp. I don't blame Damian for seeing someone behind her back. The dude was never satisfied with one woman. Babes were his second addiction, right behind drugs."

"Quite the ladies' man," Josie said sarcastically.

"How did you meet Rachel?" I asked.

He looked uncomfortable at the question. "I, uh, was

dating a friend of hers. When she introduced me to Rachel, it was love at first sight, so I dumped her."

"Such an honorable guy." Josie snorted.

Farley had the decency to look embarrassed. "Yeah, I know it was a rotten thing to do, but I had my reasons. She was a major user and wouldn't kick the habit." A muscle ticked in his jaw. "And she didn't care who it affected."

"Rachel didn't tell us about that," I said.

Farley scoffed. "Why would she? When Rachel started dating me, their friendship was toast."

Another woman scorned. Too bad it didn't lead back to Damian, because there might be a motive involved. I studied Farley's face for a moment, trying to understand the appeal. He was still an attractive enough guy, and there were no visible signs of him being a user. I honestly couldn't see him treating any woman like a queen, as Mike did for me. But Rachel, who had dated both Damian and Farley, assured us that Farley was wonderful and Damian a first-class jerk. "Is there any chance I can talk to your ex—what did you say her name was?"

Farley shook his head sadly. "No. She died last summer in an accident. She drowned."

A pang of remorse shot through me. "I'm so sorry." There was never any way to know what kind of trauma another person might be experiencing. As Grandma Rosa always said, "Never judge a book by its picture."

"Who else had a score to settle with Damian?" Josie asked. "Would his parents know of anyone?"

"Nope. His parents are both dead. He's got a brother who lives in Arizona and another in Jersey, but he hasn't seen them in years."

I thought back to the Damian I'd known in high school. Were there signs that he'd become a drug user and woman abuser? I hadn't seen any, but my grandmother obviously had. When I'd brought him over for dinner, she'd taken me aside to say that he was a bad story. She'd meant news, of course.

Farley brushed crumbs off his shirt and stood. "I've got to get back to work. Thanks for the grub."

"I hope you enjoyed them," I said with sincerity.

He wiggled a hand back and forth. "Eh. I've had better."

Josie's mouth formed a thin, hard line. She didn't take criticism well, especially where her baking skills were concerned.

"What about the two guys who carjacked me?" I asked. "How do they relate to Damian?"

He shrugged. "Damian probably owed them money. Maybe they told him if he didn't pay up, he was going to wind up dead. Damian didn't choose his contacts wisely. This kind of stuff happens every day, honey." His eyes hardened. "I warned him to get help. He was getting in too deep. Nice talking to you."

"One more thing," I said. "Do you have contact information for Magnolia?"

Farley raised an eyebrow at me. "I know where to find her, if that's what you mean. But if I were you, I'd avoid that chick."

"Why?"

He looked at me in disbelief. "Because she hates you. She's been going around telling everyone that she saw you leaving Damian's building the night he was murdered."

CHAPTER TWELVE

That was it. My Christmas goose was cooked for sure. What was to keep Magnolia from going to the police and telling them she'd seen me at Damian's? Was there any way I could stop her? Probably not. Farley said that she hated me, and she'd given every indication at the police station the other night.

Josie clicked off her cell phone. "I left a message with Dru Ann."

"Who?" I asked, distracted.

"Magnolia's sister. I asked her to let Magnolia know you wanted to see her at the bakery. We're not going to her place."

I was helping Josie with some last-minute baking for an order that had come in after Farley had left. Although it was short notice, we couldn't afford to turn down any business. A basket with 200 Christmas cookies that included macaroons, fudgy delights, gingerbread men, and chocolate cookie cups could only help our receding profit line. It was probably from someone out of town who hadn't heard that I was a potential murderess.

Dodie had slipped and twisted her ankle, and Mickey had driven her to the emergency room. Her daughter had met them there. We were relieved when Dodie called to say she was all right. She assured us she'd be back at work Monday morning. Oh, more Christmas joy.

"No Santa hunting till tomorrow, I guess," I said glumly as I popped a macaroon into my mouth. "If I'm still around tomorrow, that is."

Josie raised an eyebrow as she bent over the vanilla sugar cookies, pastry bag in hand, and created perfect swirls of fudge on top. "Stop saying that. You're having a baby, not dying."

"I'm talking about prison. Hard, iron cells. Having my baby on the cold, dirty floor with no one to help me. And what if the baby needs medical attention? They'd let me scream all night with no help."

Josie clucked her tongue. "That imagination of yours has always been vivid, but now that you're pregnant, it's off the charts. First off, you're not going to prison. Second, that scenario would *never* happen. They'd at least take you to the infirmary to have the baby."

"Well, that's a big improvement," I said tartly.

"I was arrested once, remember?" Josie asked. "Your sister would have you out on bail within five minutes. But you don't have to worry because that's *not* going to happen. It would be your word against Magnolia's, and who would believe her? She had a motive to kill Damian, and she knew he was cheating on her. Plus, she found his body. Isn't that a bit too convenient?"

"I didn't find out anything about Damian's other girlfriend or Farley's ex who died." I blew out a sigh. "My sleuthing skills have vanished."

Josie grinned. "It's all those pregnancy hormones, Nancy Drew. They fool with even the most airtight minds. No worries. I have the entire day off to hunt Santa with you tomorrow. One way or another, we'll find those Jolly-less jerks."

* * *

"But I thought you went to the mall yesterday," Mike said. It was ten o'clock on Sunday morning, and he was still in bed, which was a rarity for him. He'd complained that he might be coming down with a mild case of the flu. This had happened last week too. My grandmother told me this was common for fathers-to-be, and Mike was probably looking for some extra attention. Grandma Rosa was usually right on the money, but I was convinced that she was wrong this time.

Josie's horn honked from outside. I went to the window and held up a finger for her to wait a minute. After wrapping a wool coat around my cumbersome body, I leaned down to kiss my husband on the forehead. "No, plans changed when Dodie twisted her ankle. We won't be gone long. Josie wants to see Santa." *And so do I.*

He narrowed his eyes. "You're taking those demon kids of hers?"

"No. And they're not demons—they're sweet little boys."

"Right," he mocked and covered his eyes with his arm. "I babysat those terrors once, remember? At least *our* child won't be like that."

Oh brother. "No, I'm sure he or she will be perfect," I teased.

"I was hoping you'd stay home with me today." He uncovered his eyes and looked up at me with a pitiful expression. "I'll miss you."

Someone *was* looking for attention. Smiling, I rubbed his tousled dark head and spoke soothingly. "Don't worry. I won't be long. And I'll make you something special for dinner when I get home."

His face brightened. "Pasta fagioli?"

"Sure." Maybe my grandmother had some in her freezer. Or I could always pick up a couple of cans at the grocery store. Gee whiz, didn't he remember who he was married to? "You've been working too hard." I kissed him on the mouth, sorry for ever second-guessing my grandmother, and ran my hands down his smooth, muscular chest. He groaned.

"Okay, I'm starting to feel better. Tell Josie you've changed your mind." His eyes twinkled at me.

I laughed. "You get some rest. You never know when this little guy is going to have us on our way to the hospital. Then there will be lots of sleepless nights ahead of us."

He grabbed my hand and kissed it. "I can't wait, Sal."

"Me too." The horn sounded again. "I'll see you in a couple of hours. Love you."

"Be careful," he called after me.

There was no snow predicted for today, but the wind was in full force, whipping through my coat as I lumbered down the sidewalk and got into Josie's warm van.

"I see that baby is still sleeping on the job," Josie said cheerfully. "Hey, little dude or dudette, are you *ever* coming out to meet your Aunt Josie?"

"I'm starting to wonder the same thing myself. So, what's our game plan?" I fussed with the seat belt, stretching it as far as I could and wondering how big this baby was going to be.

Josie took a left off my street. "I checked the mall schedule online. Santa's there all today and tomorrow. I thought we'd walk up and down the concourse and see if any of his helpers looked suspicious. Maybe I should have brought one of the kids so that we could get in line to meet the real deal."

"I doubt the Santa hired to greet kids would be one of my carjackers." Call me crazy, but I couldn't imagine those gun-toting psychos being good with children.

Josie scanned the parking lot of the mall. "Man, it's jam-packed today. The last weekend before Christmas is always crazy. I think we should stop over at the costume shop too. Maybe they'd give us a list of people who rented Santa suits lately?"

I held back a laugh. "Why would they do that? Unless they thought we were cops."

"Yeah, I guess that scenario might not work for us, especially with you about to go into labor."

Josie walked swiftly toward the entrance, and I struggled to keep up. The wind left me gasping for breath, and my movements were clumsy and awkward. The baby seemed to have dropped since last night, which I knew meant he or she might come soon. I'd been so looking forward to the moment, but with everything going on, maybe it would be better if he or she stayed put for a few more days, or at least until I could prove my innocence.

A Santa Claus was standing inside the entranceway doors, ringing a bell with a Salvation Army kettle in front of him. I examined him carefully as I dropped a dollar in his red kettle. He wasn't the same one we'd seen here on Friday. This man had a pure white beard and blue eyes, while both Jolly-less Santas had brown eyes. He grinned when he noticed me staring. "Merry Christmas, ma'am."

"Merry Christmas," I repeated. When he was out of earshot, I grabbed Josie's arm. "Scratch him off the list. Have you ever seen a Santa suit with a cream-colored beard?"

She pondered my question. "It's not something I've ever

thought about before, but now that you mention it, no. Rob played Santa for the kids last year. We borrowed the suit from his coworker. It said *Dry Clean Only* on the label. I suppose if you washed it by hand or put certain parts in the washing machine, it might discolor."

"Maybe. I don't know why I'm so obsessed with the beard. That song from my childhood keeps running through my head. It goes, 'Who's got a beard that's long and white? Santa's got a beard that's long and white.'"

"I know that song. It's called 'Must Be Santa,'" Josie said. "And it doesn't say anything about having a cream-colored beard."

"Oh, whatever," I grumbled.

"It may be a lead for us," Josie said thoughtfully as we walked through the concourse and toward the customer service area. Even though it was still morning, there was already a long line of waiting parents and children. Santa was seated in his big red chair, with Mrs. Claus at his side, taking pictures and handing out candy canes.

"Want to get in line?" Josie teased.

"How? We don't have any kids with us."

Josie's gaze rested on my stomach. "Well, if you could talk that kid of yours into making a hasty appearance, we'd be all set."

"Ha-ha. I'm waiting for it to happen during Gianna's wedding." I watched as Santa lifted a pretty little girl of about six or seven onto his lap. She had long honey-colored braids that hung over her shoulders and blue eyes that shone wide in delight. My heart melted at the sight of her, and I recalled what Mike had said the other night about Christmas and believing in Santa. He was right. I couldn't hold a personal grudge against the big red man just because of what had happened to me.

"Peppermints," I said out loud.

Josie wrinkled her nose. "What?"

"One of the Jolly-less Santas smelled like peppermints. Maybe they had a stash of candy canes on them." I pointed at the silver bowl next to Santa that Mrs. Claus was reaching into. She handed one to the little girl, who started to jump up and down with excitement. "I don't think that's our guy."

"How can you be sure?" Josie asked.

"His beard is snow white. And look how good he is with the kids."

Josie raised her eyebrows. "Hey. Check it out. There goes another Mr. Ho Ho Ho."

Santa Claus's twin was walking north, back toward the main entrance. Josie was right. This mall was clearly in the business of cloning Santa. How many helpers did the real one need?

There was something familiar about this Santa as he walked, but I couldn't be positive what it was. This Santa had no padding and, as a result, was a much slimmer six-foot version. His shoulders were broad, and he walked with a proud, definitive swagger about him.

My heart started to knock against the wall of my chest. The Jolly-less Santas had also been tall, and without padding. "He could be one of them. Can you see his beard?"

She grabbed my hand. "Stop with the beard stuff. Come on. Let's follow him. I've got a weird feeling about this guy too."

I struggled to keep up with her. "Slow down!" I pleaded. "I'm not exactly a lightweight these days!" The baby gave a sharp kick and distracted me. I shook my hand loose from Josie's tight grip. "You go ahead. I can't walk that fast."

Josie stopped in front of me and swore under her breath. "Oh my God. Look at that, Sal!"

Santa had stopped for a drink at the water fountain. He was holding something in his left hand—a clear plastic bag. I squinted. "What's in it?"

"He's got a fortune cookie and gingerbread men in there!" Josie said excitedly. "*My* gingerbread men, to be exact!"

I placed a hand on my rock-hard belly. What a great time for a contraction. "If those have strawberry icing, he's got to be our guy. Remember, not all of the cookies you made that day were found with Damian's body."

"This is too much of a coincidence," Josie insisted. "And the shop is closed today. He's got to be one of them. Let me at that creep."

I tried to pull her back. "Whoa. What are you going to do? Waylay Santa in front of the entire mall? Let's follow him for a little while and see where he goes."

Josie squared her shoulders, as if prepared to do battle, and I knew I'd lost this argument. "Forget it," she said. "You stay here. I'll take care of everything."

"Jos, wait!" Another contraction hit me, and I was forced to watch as she walked swiftly toward Mr. Claus, who was now talking to a little girl and her mother. Josie ran up to him and grabbed him by the arm. When he turned around, I sucked in a breath. *Shoot.* Now I knew what was familiar about the man. With a sinking feeling of dread, I started toward them.

"Not so fast, Santa baby." Josie kept hold of his arm. "We know who you *really* are."

The woman and little girl gave Josie a funny look and hurried away. Santa glared at Josie but said nothing. My mouth went dry when Santa's angry eyes turned to meet mine and instant recognition set in. "Uh, Jos, I think we're making a mistake here."

"There's no thinking about it," a familiar male voice answered. "Of course, with you two, thinking sometimes is an afterthought. Can you guess who I am, Mrs. Sullivan?"

"Oh crap," Josie said miserably, realizing her error. This was not one of the Jolly-less Santas we were looking for. This Santa was incognito. And mad as hell.

Green eyes with golden flecks in them met mine and were filled to the brim with anger. "You two have some explaining to do," Brian said hotly.

CHAPTER THIRTEEN

―――――

Brian took Josie and me each by an arm and guided us out of the way of mall traffic. I was almost positive that I could see steam pouring out of his ears.

We were standing in front of the Lindt store, with the smell of freshly made chocolate hitting my nose like a distinct perfume. I closed my mouth to make sure I wasn't drooling and then tried to focus on what Brian was saying. It was hard to keep a straight face when you were getting reamed by Santa Claus.

"You two never give up," he growled. "All right, let's have it. What are you doing here? And don't tell me it's last-minute Christmas shopping."

Josie stuck her chin out in defiance. "We could ask you the same thing, you know. What are you doing impersonating Santa? I thought you were done with this case."

Brian's face turned the same color as his suit. "Sorry, but I'm a police officer, so *I* get to ask the questions. Maybe I should have you both arrested for interfering with a police investigation. It's been a long time coming."

"Not funny, Brian," I retorted. "Especially in light of what's happened to me the last couple of days."

"Yeah." Josie tossed her head arrogantly. "You should be used to us by now anyway."

Brian swore and shook his head. "Why am I even wasting my breath with you two? It's hopeless."

I pointed at the package of cookies in his hand. "Those are our gingerbread men. The shop isn't open today, so when we saw you carrying them—"

"You immediately jumped to conclusions, like you always do." Brian scowled and took off his Santa hat, running a hand through his dirty blond hair in frustration. "If you must know, a little girl brought them for me. She said that she wanted to give me cookies now, in case I had too many to eat on Christmas Eve. Then she told me that they came from her favorite bakery in the whole world—Sally's Samples."

I beamed with pride. "Oh, that's so sweet."

Josie's eyes scanned the mall. "Where is this kid? We could use her for publicity. The shop hasn't exactly been doing well the last couple of days, especially since Sal's considered a murder suspect."

"One last time," Brian said in a somewhat strangled tone. "What are you both doing here?"

I gave in. "Oh, fine. We're looking for the Jolly-less Santas. From your getup, I'm guessing that you're doing the same thing."

Brian was silent for a beat before answering. Maybe he was counting to ten in his head, an attempt to keep from strangling us. "It's entirely possible. But the fact remains that you two have no business being here."

My temper flared. "Oh, come off it. What did you expect me to do, Brian? You said you were taking yourself off the case. You're the only one at the station who's always had my back. Was I supposed to wait until someone identified me going into Damian's building the night he was murdered? And then what—you come and arrest me while I'm in the delivery room?"

Brian and Josie both stared at me with a puzzled expression. "Sal, what are you talking about?" she asked.

That damned dream again. Heat crept up my neck. "Nothing," I murmured.

"We thought this would be a good place to find Sal's carjackers," Josie explained. "Let's face it, Brian—this place has more Santas then Mrs. Gavelli has black housecoats."

His mouth twitched at the corners, then he cleared his throat and shot me the evil eye. "Regardless, you shouldn't be here snooping around, Sally. You're nine months pregnant, for God's sake!"

"I don't have a choice. There's no reason to worry. I'm not taking any unnecessary chances."

"Yeah, right," Brian mumbled. "Let's face it—your

middle name is disaster."

I ignored his rather rude comment. "Have you found out anything to help me?"

He rubbed a hand over his phony beard and sighed. "Not yet. I wanted off the case, but we're shorthanded, so my boss said I had no choice. I've been going around talking to fellow Santas today. We're making progress."

"What kind of progress?" I was a bit miffed that he wasn't back on the case by his own accord. "Have you looked into where the Santa suits may have come from? Can you check out the costume store in town to see if they were rented there?"

He gave me a look of disbelief. "Sally, do you think this is my first day on the job? Of course I've already checked there. We tracked down every suit that's been rented or bought at the costume shop on Starwood Avenue since before Thanksgiving."

Shoot. Another dead end. I leaned my head against the bric-a-brac design of the Lindt store wall, the smell comforting me despite my depression. "I didn't mean to insult you, but I'm desperate here. Is there any other place in town that rents Santa suits?"

Brian frowned. "Not that I can recall. We're wondering if—"

Josie put a hand to her mouth. "Wait a second! I forgot all about Candy."

"Who?" Then it dawned on me. "Oh! I forgot too!"

Brian looked at both of us like we had corn growing out of our ears. "Who or what is Candy?"

"Candy Stevens," I replied. "She's a customer of ours who owns a little store that specializes in holiday fare, Party Hardy. She sells costumes for Halloween and even some for the Fourth of July. I'm betting she'd have Santa suits."

Josie drew out her phone. "Why not? She has everything else. And her stuff is cheaper than the costume stores. Candy ordered a tray of cookies last week, so I've got her number in here somewhere." She scrolled through her contacts list, pressed the screen, and waited. "Hi, Candy? Josie Sullivan here. I need a favor."

"This makes perfect sense," I told Brian. "Why not go to a smaller store? Would you need a subpoena to get their credit card information?"

"If they used a credit card," Brian said. "Since it's a small store and she owns it, no. Candy doesn't have to give me the original records without a subpoena, but a copy will suit me fine. If they were smart, they'd have paid cash, so don't get your hopes up."

"Well, they didn't seem very bright to me," I admitted.

Brian raised his eyebrows. "The owner of the jewelry store they held up uttered the same sentiment. They asked him for a bag to haul away the money in his cash register."

I shook my head in disbelief. The baby moved, and I placed a hand on my belly, bracing for another contraction, but nothing came. "This makes me think that someone else was involved and engineering the robberies. These guys were puppets on a string, so to speak."

Brian looked impressed. "Well done, Mrs. Donovan. I happen to think the same thing. Given your current condition, though, it seems that my job is safe for a few weeks."

"Very funny," I said.

Josie covered her phone with her hand and addressed Brian. "I think we hit pay dirt. Candy said she had two suits in stock and rented them both at the beginning of December. She looked up the sale while I was waiting and said they used a credit card. If you want to give her a couple of minutes, she can fax over the receipt to you or text it. She can't give you the original copy though."

Brian put his hand out for the phone. "That's fine. Let me talk to Candy. I'll tell her where to send the information. If there's a hotline number associated with the card, we might be able to get an address within the hour—if we're lucky, that is."

* * *

We parted ways with Brian shortly afterward. He promised to keep us in the loop on his search for the Jolly-less Santas, and I was relieved that our sleuthing was done for the day. My back ached from walking, and the smell of chocolate had driven me to such distraction that I'd gone into the Lindt store for an impromptu purchase. A half hour later and forty dollars poorer, I'd emerged with every kind of truffle imaginable, from peppermint cookie to caramel to red velvet.

Josie grinned and shook her head as she opened the van door for me. I held my bag of goodies out to her as she got behind the wheel. "Have some."

"No thanks." She laughed and pointed at my belly. "I can see the baby moving. Guess someone else is enjoying them too."

"He's going to look like his father but take after his mother and her love of sweets. Chocolate always makes me happy, even when I'm a murder suspect." I reached into the bag for a hot chocolate-flavored candy. "We need to make truffle-flavored cookies."

Josie pointed at the windshield. "Check it out. Officer Hottie looks like he's on a mission."

I glanced up in time to see Brian exiting the mall, in full police uniform, with a duffel bag under one arm and his phone pressed to his ear. Adam was by his side. They hurried to the cruiser parked by the front door and sped off, lights flashing. "Holy cow. Do you think they could have found the Santas?"

Josie grinned wickedly at me as she started the engine. "Let's follow them."

Uneasiness shot through me like a cold gust of wind. "Jos, if they see us, Brian's going to be furious. And I promised to stay out of it."

"Aw, what's the harm?" Josie asked. "We'll stay in the van. Don't you want to see if they find the delinquents who almost killed you?"

I did, but I'd also promised Mike that I wouldn't take any unnecessary chances and intended to keep my word. "Maybe you'd better take me home."

Josie acted like she hadn't heard me and ran a yellow light. "We'll only stay a couple of minutes. Scout's honor."

"You were never a Girl Scout," I reminded her.

"True, but I wanted to be one. Once. At least for a day, I think." She took a left down a one-way street. "It still counts, right?"

There was a car in between ours and Brian's, so I didn't think he'd seen us. The emergency lights on his cruiser suddenly went off as we approached a three-story brick apartment building that looked like it might crumble to the ground at any second.

"They must be here for another reason. You're telling me that the Jolly-less Santas live less than ten minutes from the bakery? And no one's been able to find them?"

"Last I heard, they were supposed to condemn this building," Josie remarked. She guided the vehicle into a parking space near the rear entrance. A blue van with the apartment complex's name and logo on it was directly in front of us, and it shielded us partially from Brian and Adam's view.

Josie rolled down her window and stretched her body through it, peering around the van. "They just rang the bell and shouted something into the speaker, but I can't make out what. The door opened for them."

"Why are those Santas living in this dump if they've been robbing every store in Colwestern?" I asked. "Are they sitting on all this money?"

"Maybe because no one would think to look for them here," Josie said thoughtfully. "Or they're staying with a friend. It might be the perfect hide out."

My chest tightened. It bothered me that I couldn't see what was happening, and the entire situation was becoming scary. "We should leave."

"Let's wait a minute," Josie said, distracted by the pinging of her phone. She glanced down at the screen and pursed her lips. "That husband of mine. All he thinks about is what's for dinner. Doesn't he know we have more important things to do?" Annoyed, she quickly began to type out a message.

I was getting a bad feeling about this. Josie and I had been in similar situations before, and I wanted to avoid another. I had no intention of taking any chances with my unborn child. My nerves set another contraction in motion, and I tried to breathe through it as fast as I could.

Josie glanced sharply at me. "You okay, love?"

I managed a quick nod. "Another Braxton Hicks, I think. Look, Brian will call me later if he has any news. I want to go home and—"

A click sounded, and we both turned our heads. On Josie's side of the van was the big red man himself, sporting a cream-colored beard, with a gun pointed at Josie.

Icicles formed between my shoulder blades. *No, please. Not again.* "Oh my God," I whispered. "It's him."

Josie didn't reply. My normally outspoken friend had been frozen into immobility as she stared down the barrel of his gun. Santa Claus was surely going to be the death of me.

"Ho, ho, ho," Santa greeted us. The smell of peppermints wafted through the cold air and sent a chill down my spine. "I'm in a bit of a hurry, so get out of the van quick, and I'll let you live."

Josie started to shake, but she made no attempt to move. I touched her arm lightly. "Jos? Let's do as he says, all right?"

A stream of four-letter expletives fell out of Santa's mouth as he brought the gun to the side of my friend's head. "I said get out of the van. Now!"

Santa was short on patience today, but at least it seemed to draw Josie out of her trance. "O-kay," Josie murmured. "Just give me a second."

I stared wide-eyed at Santa as Josie unbuckled her seat belt. Yes, he was the one who had shoved me into the snow, I was certain of it. But where was his partner? Still inside the building? Under arrest? Had they seen the police car approaching and gone into panic mode?

Santa had clearly had enough of our stalling tactics. He yanked the door open, grabbed Josie roughly by the arm, and threw her to the ground. She fell to her knees on the parking lot blacktop.

"Hey!" Josie screamed. "Don't hurt my friend. She's pregnant!"

He turned his head and seemed to see me for the first time. More expletives followed. "Oh no. Not you again!"

Now it was my turn to sit there, frozen. This was a horrifying déjà vu no one should ever have to experience once, let alone twice. Shaking, I put my hand on the door to push it open just as Santa hauled Josie to her feet then pointed the gun at her head. "Get out of the van, fatso, unless you want me to shoot your friend."

Josie stared at me with fearful eyes. My hand still rested on the door handle, the other on my purse.

"I mean it," he warned and then muttered another

obscenity at me. "Do as I say, or I'll shoot Red here."

My heart was in my throat. I prayed Brian and Adam would emerge from the building any second. I held up my right hand while my left one managed to press the contact button for Brian's phone.

Santa waved the gun in my direction. "Get out of the van!" he screamed.

"Sally?" I could faintly hear Brian's voice come on the line.

I held up both my hands and spoke loudly, for Brian's benefit. "All right. I'm opening the door now."

Santa gave Josie a push that sent her halfway across the lot. He got into her side of the van and tried to push me out of the door as a male voice shouted, "Let her go!"

We both looked up. Brian and Adam were standing a few feet away from the van. The other Santa was between them, sporting a pair of handcuffs. Before I could get out of the van, Santa wrapped an arm around my neck and held the gun against my head.

"Damn it, Leroy! Don't you dare open your mouth to those pigs, or we're both dead for sure!" Santa screamed into my ear.

"I didn't tell them nothin', Lyle," Leroy insisted. "I swear. They don't know about the orders."

"Keep your mouth shut!" Adam told him sternly.

The gun shook at the side of my head, and I didn't dare breathe. I glanced helplessly out the windshield at Brian. He stared back at me, concern evident on his face. One false move and I was done for—along with my poor innocent child. I had tried to be careful. Why did these things always happen to me?

Brian kept his gun aimed at Lyle. "Drop the gun, and move away from her," he said in a strangely calm voice.

Lyle shook his head. "No way, man. You let Leroy go first, or she's dead." He pressed the barrel of the gun into my skull.

A lump of fear the size of a mountain grew in my throat. There was nothing I could do but pray that somehow Brian would get me out of this.

Seemingly of its own accord, the van's engine started.

Lyle jumped in his seat, startled by the action as if someone had electrocuted him. He moved the gun away from me as I wasted no time pushing the door open and half falling, half stumbling to the pavement below. A succession of shots sounded as I lay on the blacktop, curled in a fetal position, my arms protectively around my belly, listening to Josie scream.

After a few seconds, all went quiet, and I forced myself to look up into the van's interior. Lyle was slumped sideways onto my seat, a steady stream of blood oozing from his head.

Brian ran toward me, but Josie had already reached my side and wrapped her arms around me. He stepped around us to check on Lyle. When he turned around and his gaze met mine, I knew the man was dead. Brian radioed for backup while Adam led a screaming Leroy into the back of the squad car.

"Oh my God, Sal!" Josie wept. "Are you hurt?"

I managed to shake my head no, my gaze still fixated on Lyle's body.

"Is he—" Josie faltered as she looked at Brian, who had squatted down next to me.

"Yeah. He's dead." Brian blew out a sigh and looked over at Adam, who was now trying to hold back a small crowd of people who had emerged from the apartment building. He stared into my eyes, the grief palpable in his own.

Josie noticed his expression as they both helped me to my feet. "Are *you* all right?"

"It's the first time I've ever killed someone." Brian's voice shook and was barely above a whisper. He stared down at the gun in his hand and then, as if he couldn't bear to look at it again, hastily shoved the weapon into his belt. Despite the terror and shock at what had happened to me, my heart ached for him.

Josie sobbed as she hugged me against her. "Oh, Sal. This is all my fault. Please forgive me. It was a stupid thing to do!"

"It was *your* idea to come here?" Brian asked sharply.

Tears streamed down Josie's face. "Yes, I made Sal come with me. She didn't want to."

Brian's mouth hardened in a firm, thin line. "I'm pretty pissed off at you, but I'll admit that it was a smart thing to turn that car starter on at just the right moment. You saved Sally's life."

Josie's large blue eyes looked as if someone had watered them down. "But I didn't," she wailed. "I'd have been too afraid it might backfire. The starter—I forgot it was in my pocket when I stuck my hand inside. I must have set it off by accident."

My body was still reeling from shock, and I was thankful for Josie's arm around my waist, supporting me. It took a moment to comprehend what she was saying. "Wai—wait a min-minute. You mean, you didn't set it off on purpose?"

She shook her head. "I wish I could say I did. I'm just thankful it worked out."

Sirens screamed in the distance, growing louder as they got closer. Nausea rumbled in my belly as I grabbed it between my hands.

"Oh, Sal, that had to be such a shock to your system. Do you think you're in labor?" Josie asked.

The baby kicked at that moment, and I managed a small smile. "No. I'm starting to think this baby is never coming out."

CHAPTER FOURTEEN

———

Grandma Rosa watched me curiously as I set my phone down on the kitchen table. "What did Mike have to say?"

I hesitated. It wasn't what Mike had said—it was actually *how* he'd said it. He'd gone bananas when he found out what had happened. "Not much. He, ah, is on his way over to get me."

"Oh yes. I can imagine that he is." Grandma Rosa's soulful brown eyes regarded me with sympathy as she set a cup of hot chocolate topped with homemade whipped cream in front of me.

I blew out a sigh and stared at the picture on the side of the mug—a Santa climbing out of a house chimney. No sense trying to fight it. The big red man was everywhere.

I took a long sip of the drink and then wrapped my hands around the mug, comforted by its warmth. I stared up at the cheerful walls of my parents' kitchen, painted the same color as the sun. I'd once run my bakery out of this room for a brief time, when there had been a fire at my shop and no other location available. It was bright and warm and always immaculate since my grandmother spent most of her day here.

The bottle of anisette on the Formica countertop caught my eye, sitting all by its lonely self. That would have been a comfort too. I'd never been much of a drinker, but if I wasn't pregnant, I may have been tempted to add some to my hot chocolate.

Grandma Rosa followed my gaze and raised an eyebrow in question. She'd been surprised when I showed up on my parents' doorstep. I'd purposefully asked Brian to bring me here instead of my house. Mike was going to be furious and upset, thinking that I'd lied to him about staying out of trouble, and that hadn't been my intention. "I'm using you, Grandma."

She shot me a puzzled look. "I do not understand. How are you using me?"

I put my head in my hands. "Mike will be so upset at me and at Josie, especially if he finds out she's the reason we were at the apartment complex. If you're here, he might not yell." Or perhaps not as loudly. "I don't want him to hate Josie for this, so I'm half tempted to say it was my idea."

Grandma Rosa's eyes widened. "No, *cara mia*. Do not lie. You must tell him that Josie took you there."

"But, Grandma—" I protested.

She wagged a finger in my face. "Never tell a lie to your husband. Well, to anyone, really. Besides, Mike must realize by now that trouble—well, it just seems to find you. No matter how much you try to behave, *cara mia*, I am afraid it will never leave you."

I blew out a breath, thinking the same thing. "Did you ever lie to Grandpa?"

"Eh." She wiggled her hand back and forth. "A couple of times. Once when your mother was dating your father. She was only nineteen and your father thirty-two when they began seeing each other. A big age difference back then, and your grandfather did not like your father either."

That part I already knew. "But you were okay with it?"

She put a finger to the side of her short white hair and twirled it around. "I knew from the beginning that your father was *pazza*, but what could I do? Your mother loved him, and I wanted her to be happy. As the saying goes, I turned a closed eye to it."

"That's blind eye, Grandma."

"Whatever." She stirred her coffee, and a wistful look came onto her face. "Of course, I told other lies that I am not proud of as well. Lies that had nothing to do with your mother and father. Remember how I told you the story of the young man I was in love with before I met your grandfather?"

"Vernon."

She smiled, pleased that I had remembered his name. Grandma Rosa had been seventeen to his twenty-three years when they met. Like my grandfather, her father thought Vernon was too old for his daughter. Being an old-school Italian, he had refused to let Grandma Rosa see the man, so they had met in secret.

"He went away to the Vietnam War, and you never heard from him again."

"He died," Grandma Rosa said sadly.

"But you don't know for certain," I pointed out, hating to see her unhappy. "Perhaps he's still alive. Maybe he had an injury and—"

Grandma Rosa cut me off. "No. He is dead. I can feel it in my heart." She patted my cheek. "Ah, *cara mia*. Always such the optometrist."

She sighed, and I didn't bother to correct her this time. A dreamy look came into her eyes, which surprised me. My grandmother was not a dreamer. She was too practical and didn't have time for it. She was always cooking or crocheting or giving someone valuable advice.

For a moment, the lines faded from her face as she stared over my shoulder in silence. How I wish I had known her when she was younger. I'd seen black and white photos of her with the saddle shoes and poodle skirts that had dominated the 1950s, when she was a teenager. She had been beautiful, with long, black curly locks like my own and large brown eyes that sparkled with a bit of mischief. I suspected that she'd been a bit like Josie back then—a regular spitfire.

"I hope my child will be just like you," I said with all sincerity.

She smiled and went to the stove to turn the kettle off. "Your child will not be like anyone else, *cara mia*. She or he will always belong to themselves. A free spirit." Her eyes twinkled. "But I do think there is a little bit of me in you. We are both survivors. Never forget that."

My grandmother had been through so much in her life. After she'd given birth to my mother, the doctor had warned her not to have any more children. She'd worked as a nurse until she'd married my grandfather and then taken care of him when he'd fallen ill with cancer. She was an excellent cook and could crotchet or knit anything asked of her. I'd never had a hobby or craft I was very good at and could barely make decent cookies compared to Josie's. Maybe solving murders was supposed to be my calling in life in addition to being a mother. After today's latest episode, though, I wasn't sure how much more I could take. Suddenly I felt very tired.

The front door slammed, and I braced myself. Mike had been in the shower when I called, but he'd said he'd be over immediately. I was not looking forward to his lecture.

Gianna appeared in the doorway, her face white and drawn as if she'd seen a ghost. Her chestnut-colored hair, which always fell in perfect waves around her shoulders, looked as if she'd run a rake through it. "Grandma." Her voice quavered, and then she spotted me sitting at the table. "Sal! Is everything okay?"

"Your sister was almost carjacked again," Grandma Rosa said quietly, "but the police saved her in time. Oh, and she saw a man shot to death." She shrugged and raised the kettle in the air. "It is just another ordinary day in Sally's life. Would you like tea?"

"Oh my God!" Gianna hurried over to sit in Grandma Rosa's discarded chair. "What happened?"

"I'm okay," I assured her as she put her arms around me. Then I drew back to study her face. "But you're not. What's wrong? Is it about the wedding?"

Gianna's chocolate brown eyes filled with tears, and my heart stopped for a moment. "Sweetheart, what's wrong?"

Gianna accepted a tissue and cup of tea from Grandma. "Dad. Need I say more? He's really done it this time."

Oh boy. I'd been expecting her to say Mrs. Gavelli instead. "Let me guess. He's having a book signing during the reception?"

"Not even close." Gianna wiped at her eyes.

Before she could continue, the front door opened, and I winced. "That must be Mike." I held on to Gianna's hand, as much for her support as mine.

My father and mother walked into the kitchen, their hands full of bags from the local Party Warehouse store.

Gianna swallowed a mouthful of the hot liquid placed before her and then sucked in a sharp breath as she stared apprehensively at the bags. "Dad, I need to talk to you."

"Look, honey." My mother giggled. "We picked up the wedding favors you ordered."

"But I didn't order any favors," Gianna protested, then clamped a hand over her mouth. "Oh God. Nicoletta did this, didn't she?"

My father proudly held up one of the favors. It was a small plastic bottle of oregano with Johnny's and Gianna's names and wedding date on the front, draped by a red bow the same color as my shapeless dress.

I squinted at the smaller writing underneath their names. "What does the rest of it say?"

My mother raised an eyebrow as she read the words aloud. "'May your marriage always have Italian flavor.' Hmm. Well, I guess it's kind of cute."

Gianna looked as if she wanted to shoot someone. "I can't believe she went ahead and ordered those tacky things behind my back. I told her we were going to have champagne bottles at everyone's plate, not bottles of oregano!" She pointed an accusatory finger at my father. "And I know what *you* did! About the so-called limo!"

"What?" My father looked confused. "Oh, *that*. Hey, weddings are expensive, sweetheart. Besides, it's at night. No one will ever tell the difference."

Uh-oh. I had an idea what might have happened and prayed to be wrong.

Gianna's lower lip trembled. "You had one job, Dad. One job! How could you do this to me?"

Grandma Rosa shook her head and sighed. "Your father, he is more *pazza* than I thought."

"Hey," my father protested. "I'm not crazy. Limos cost a fortune, and there's nothing wrong with using a black vehicle instead of a white one."

I brought a hand to my mouth. "Only it's not a limo, is it, Dad?" He didn't answer, and I continued. "You hired a hearse to bring them to the church, didn't you?"

He grinned. "Nope. That's the best part. I didn't have to hire it. I got it for free from Phibbins Mortuary. I even got two so that the rest of us can ride in comfort as well!"

"That is never going to happen," Grandma Rosa

announced.

My father went on as if he hadn't heard her. "They were more than happy to supply the vehicles. Since they advertise on my blog, I'm giving them a free space next week in return. And don't worry, honey. They assured me there won't be any dead bodies in the back."

"That does it!" Gianna screamed. "I will *not* go to my wedding in a *hearse*!"

"Nicoletta thought it was a good idea too," my father said. "She thinks there might even be some old Italian tradition about it bringing the bride and groom luck."

Gianna stood and grabbed her coat. "Then you and Nicoletta ride in it. I'm done. This is my day, and I'm not going to be made a laughingstock. The wedding is off!"

She rushed from the room. I started to get up and go after her, but my mother beat me to it. "Gianna! Wait, honey!"

I could hear my sister sobbing as she slammed the front door.

Grandma Rosa glared at my father. "I knew this was going to happen. All because you and that *pazza* woman next door cannot mind your own business."

"When's dinner?" my father asked, as if nothing were wrong. "All that shopping has made me hungry."

"I don't believe this," I said. "Your daughter just called off her wedding! Aren't you going to run after her?"

My father helped himself to one of Grandma Rosa's candy cane brownies on the Christmas tree platter in the center of the table. "Nah. She didn't mean it. Besides, she would lose the deposit on the hall." He took a bite and chewed thoughtfully. "Needs more peppermint, Rosa. Maybe add some Schnapps next time too." He stood, gave me a pat on the head, and whistled cheerfully as he went into the living room.

"I would like to Schnapp *you*," Grandma Rosa called after him. She grabbed oven mitts to take the lasagna out of the oven. The delicious smell was warm, inviting, and soothing. Most of the time I couldn't eat when I was upset, but things had been different since my pregnancy.

The front door slammed again, and Mike flew into the kitchen like a blast of cold wind. He stooped to his knees and put his arms around me. "Sal! Are you all right, baby?"

"I'm okay." I leaned my head on his shoulder, comforted by the feel of him. "*We're* okay, I mean."

Mike put a hand on my belly, and I covered it with mine. He studied my face for a moment, and then his mouth curved into a slight frown. "Why did you lie to me, Sal?"

The hurt was obvious in his husky tone, and sorrow imminent in those midnight blue eyes that I adored so much, making me want to weep. I had expected screaming and would have preferred it to this. Tears welled in the corners of my eyes. "But I didn't."

"You promised me that you'd stay out of trouble. You said you'd call me if you needed help."

Grandma Rosa regarded us in silence. I knew she was waiting to see what I would say and if I would bring up Josie's name. Heck, *I* was waiting to see what I would say too. "Uh—"

Mike brought my hand to his lips. "You should have called me when Josie wouldn't leave."

"Huh?" I was confused.

"Josie phoned me after you did," Mike explained. "She was crying and said it was all her fault that you guys were at that complex in the first place. She said you wanted to go home, but she was curious to see what might happen. I'm sorry for yelling at you on the phone, princess, but I was so scared." His voice broke. "I don't know what I'd do if something happened to you or our baby. You two are my entire world."

Tears slid down my face as I wrapped my arms around his neck. We held each other for a couple of minutes in silence, and when we finally separated, I noticed that my grandmother had discreetly left the room.

"I'm fine," I told Mike again. "I called the doctor, and he said there was no reason to come in if the baby was still moving and I wasn't in any pain. Josie didn't mean to put me in any danger. One of the Santas is dead and the other in custody, so this nightmare is close to being over." At least I hoped so.

Mike cupped my face between his hands. "What else? Did one of them kill Damian?"

"I'm not sure. Brian promised to call me after he had talked to the Santa in custody, Leroy. His partner, Lyle, was taken to the morgue."

Grandma Rosa returned. "I have some pasta fagioli for you, Mike," she said. "That should help you feel better. Sally said you had the flu." She winked at me knowingly.

Mike's face reddened slightly. "Thanks, Rosa. That sounds great." He sat down in the chair next to mine and rubbed his eyes wearily. "Well, at least you're not a suspect anymore, right?"

"I don't think so." It seemed unlikely, but who knew for certain? In the past, I'd been a potential victim more times than a suspect. From being locked in a sauna, to tied up and left for dead in an apartment with the gas on, to shut up in a freezer with a killer, I thought I must have seen it all by now. As Mike often said, I was like a cat with nine lives. The sad part was that sometimes I wondered how many I had left.

"I'm not convinced those guys killed Damian." My intuition was telling me that someone else had done the deed. "Remember the note I found in my car? There has to be another person involved or calling the shots, and maybe they killed him as well."

"Maybe." Mike sat back in his chair. "Look, I'm sorry the guy died, but all I care about is that my wife and baby aren't involved in this train wreck anymore. It was ridiculous that Brian even considered you a suspect."

"My cake server and cookies were at the crime scene," I reminded him. "Someone wanted me to take the blame, but why? And who?" That person was out there somewhere and still might have it in for me.

Mike frowned. "I know how that beautiful mind is working, princess. Let the police find Damian's killer. It's what they get paid for. My wife has more important things to accomplish—like bringing our child into this world." He winked.

I smiled but said nothing. Perhaps Mike didn't realize that until the killer was caught, it would still affect the bakery's profits at our busiest time of the year. It was only three days until Christmas, and we'd had many last-minute cancellations. We were usually swamped up until New Year's Day. Would people start to show up, or would the gossip mill concerning Sally's Shambles continue to turn? I was betting on the latter. People in

Colwestern needed to find a different hobby to keep them entertained.

  Mike gratefully accepted a cup of tea from Grandma Rosa. "What about Josie's van? Is it drivable?"

  I spooned some whipped cream into my mouth. "The windows need to be replaced, and the van needs to be cleaned, but other than that, I think it's fine. The police won't release it to her yet though. Fortunately, she can use her mother-in-law's car in the meantime. If not, I would have lent her mine."

  The front door slammed again. Grandma Rosa sighed as she carried the crystal salad bowl to the dining room table. "It is like Grand Central Station in here today."

  Brian strode into the room, his expression grim as he nodded to us. "Your mother said it was okay to come in."

  Mike slowly rose from his chair, and for a moment, I wasn't sure what to expect, thanks to Gianna's outburst the other day. I should have trusted my husband more. He extended his hand for Brian to shake, as he'd done in the hospital after my carjacking. "You saved Sal's life today. I can't thank you enough."

  Brian's face reddened. "You're welcome, but I was only doing my job. There's no need for thanks." He cocked an eyebrow at me. "You're no longer a suspect of course. And I hope you realize that I never considered you one, not even for a moment. But that doesn't change the fact that you ladies shouldn't have been there today."

  I didn't attempt to defend myself. Let him go ahead and blow off some steam at my expense. The baby, Josie, and I were okay, and that was all that mattered. Josie had admitted the entire situation was her fault, and Mike was no longer angry. Hopefully, things could get back to normal. I gestured for Brian to sit down. "What did Leroy tell you?"

  Brian looked exhausted as he sank into a chair. "Not much. Leroy clearly couldn't think for himself and did whatever Lyle told him to. Leroy has the brawn, but no brains. Not that Lyle was a genius either. There was definitely someone else who orchestrated the robberies and gave them the order to kill Damian."

  This wasn't news to me. "But who?"

"Your guess is as good as mine," Brian said wearily. "Leroy didn't even know if it was a man or woman. Lyle always talked to the 'Head Elf,' which is the name they gave this person."

"Are you serious?" This was getting weirder by the moment. "Is it possible that Leroy is lying and *does* know who the killer is?"

"Doubtful." Brian shrugged. "He's not smart enough to concoct a story like that, trust me. And we don't know for sure that the Head Elf was the one to kill Damian. Someone else might be involved."

"Unbelievable." Who could this Head Elf person be, and did they have a personal connection to Damian? One of the Santas was in custody and the other dead, but we still knew nothing about the killer. It was impossible to rest easy until that person was also behind bars.

Someone had tried to frame me. I had no connections to Damian except for my brief infatuation with him 16 years ago. But he'd told everyone and their grandmother that I still had it "bad" for him. If the Head Elf had been looking to make someone else a patsy, I was the perfect applicant for the job. All that was needed to incriminate me was for the killer to break into my bakery, steal some personal items, and plant them next to the body. Easy peasy.

Mike squeezed my hand. "You can leave it alone now, baby. Those psycho Santas won't be bothering you anymore."

He was right. It was best to leave it alone. Brian had assured me I was no longer a suspect, and the police would find Damian's killer eventually. So, why did I worry that the killer still had me in their sights?

CHAPTER FIFTEEN

———

For the first time in days, I slept like a log. There were no more worries of being arrested in the delivery room or birthing my child behind iron bars. Damian's killer was still on the loose, but I had to let it go. My child had already been in enough danger to last him or her a lifetime. I looked forward to spending the holiday with my husband and child—whenever he or she decided to arrive, that was.

When I awoke, it was after eleven o'clock, and Mike was setting a breakfast tray on the bed. He'd made me pancakes, sausages, and a cup of coffee at full caffeine strength. "You need it," he said when I protested. "Your grandmother said that this late in the pregnancy isn't going to harm the baby."

Grandma Rosa's word had always been golden for me. I polished off the pancakes and sausages in record time while he lay on the bed next to me, running his hand over my belly and smiling up at me. "What? Haven't you ever seen a fat lady eat before?" I teased.

He kissed me on the forehead. "You're not fat. You're the most beautiful woman in the world."

I sighed. "You always say the right thing, Mr. Donovan. Say, how's that flu treating you today? All better now?"

Mike waved a hand in the air, as if brushing it off. "Oh, I kicked it out in no time. No big deal. And knowing that my wife is no longer a suspect in a drug addict's murder made a huge difference."

Oh yeah. Grandma Rosa had been right, but then again, she always was.

Mike winked. "It's only two days till Christmas. There's still plenty of time for our little person to arrive before the big day."

We both watched my belly moving and laughed. "He's finishing breakfast," I said.

Mike raised an eyebrow at me. "You mean *she*, not *he*."

"Nope, you're wrong. It's definitely a boy."

"Maybe you should ask the fortune cookies what the baby's sex is." Mike grinned and rolled off the bed before I could smack him. He picked up my empty tray and whistled cheerfully as he went down the hall with it.

My phone buzzed from the nightstand, and an unknown number popped up on the screen. "Hello?"

"Yeah. This is Magnolia. Farley said you wanted to see me."

I'd forgotten all about her. "Oh, hi. Thanks for getting in touch."

"Look, I heard about those guys getting caught—you know, the ones that wanted to kill Damian." Her voice was childlike, not shrill and loud as I remembered at the police station the other day. "I'm sorry for telling the cops you did it, but it was *your* knife next to his body."

"Cake server, not knife," I corrected. "And I told you that I was set up. Why in the world would I have wanted him dead—because he embarrassed me 16 years ago? That's crazy."

"All right, I get your point." She paused. "Can we still meet?"

Confused, I stared at the phone. "There's no need to anymore, is there?"

She was silent for several seconds. "I'm afraid the police think I might have done it."

Gee, why would they ever think that? Magnolia might have been the one to find Damian's body, but that didn't mean anything. She could have staged it all after she killed him. Maybe Magnolia had broken into my shop, stabbed her boyfriend with the server, placed the gingerbread at the crime scene, and then called the police. "I'm no longer involved. This has nothing to do with me anymore."

"That's where you're wrong," she said. "Whoever killed Damian framed you. They may still come after you."

Her words chilled me. Magnolia was smarter than I'd

thought.

"Look, I don't trust those pigs," she went on. "They keep acting like I killed Damian. I could never hurt anyone. We didn't have a perfect relationship, but I still loved him. They think I know those two morons who carjacked you, but I don't, honest to God."

"Magnolia, like I told you—"

She cut me off. "There's some things about Damian that you don't know, which might help convince you that I didn't kill him."

"Magnolia, why do you care what I think? My words don't carry any clout with the police." If anything, they were sick of the sight of me.

"I've heard about your reputation—you know, solving murder cases before the cops did," Magnolia explained. "Also, that you've found a dead body or two."

Or ten. I sensed disaster waiting to happen but was curious about what Magnolia had to say. No, I wouldn't go to meet her anywhere she suggested, but I'd be safe at the bakery with Josie. "All right. Can you meet me at my bakery this afternoon? Maybe around two o'clock?"

Magnolia inhaled and then exhaled into the phone, which made me think she was puffing away on a cigarette. "Yeah. I'll be there. And no cops." She clicked off without another word.

I lumbered out of bed and went to take a shower. As I was getting dressed, Mike came back into the bedroom and stood there, hands on hips. "Time to go?"

The overanxious father. He looked so darned cute that I couldn't help but laugh. "No, silly. I'm going to the bakery for a little while. I'll only be gone for about an hour or so."

His dark blue eyes narrowed. "Sal, what's really going on? I thought you were done with work."

He deserved to know the truth, but he wasn't going to like it. "Magnolia wants to meet with me. Don't worry. Josie will be there and the customers, so—"

Mike's fists clenched at his sides. "No way in hell. She could be Damian's killer, Sal."

"I'm aware of that. Magnolia said she had some things to

tell me. Besides, it's going to be in broad daylight, and there will be people around. Anyway, I want to see if business has picked up any."

"You could always text Josie and ask about the sales." Worry lines creased his forehead. "The only way I'll let you go is if I'm with you."

"Fine." I raised my face to kiss his. "You're awfully cute when you're mad, Mr. Donovan."

He tried to look stern, but failed, his mouth twitching into a smile. "Grab your coat while I warm up the truck."

When we arrived at the bakery, I was disappointed to see that there were only two customers in the store. Josie waved to us from behind the counter as she rang up an order. I stifled a groan. Two days before Christmas the place should have been mobbed with people buying gingerbread men, Christmas tree sugar cookies, snickerdoodles, and jelly cookies. We couldn't seem to catch a break.

Mike must have guessed my thoughts, because his arm tightened around my shoulders. "Don't worry, princess. They'll all come rushing in at the last minute."

After the customers left, Josie came over to greet us. "How are you feeling, Sal? Any bruises from yesterday?"

Mike frowned. "Bruises? From what?"

I shot Josie a warning glance. Mike didn't know about my tumble out of the van. It had only been a slight fall, but I'd still managed a cut on my leg that he hadn't seen. "Ah, Santa grabbed my wrist a little too tight, but I'm fine."

A muscle ticked in Mike's jaw, but he said nothing. I worried that he might scare Magnolia off when she arrived. "Sweetheart, why don't you sit in the truck when Magnolia gets here?"

Josie's mouth opened in amazement. "She's coming here? Why?"

"She said she has some things to tell me about Damian that might help," I replied.

"I don't like this," Mike declared. "What if she has a gun? I'm not leaving you, Sal."

Josie's eyes misted over. She must still be hurting over what had happened. "Mike, I'm so sorry about yesterday. There's no way I'd ever let that woman hurt Sal. I won't leave her side." She pulled out her cell and flicked on the video option. "I'm recording the entire conversation."

Good grief. "Between the two of you, we'll be lucky if Magnolia doesn't run screaming out of here. She only wants to talk, and I'd like to know who set me up. Sure, Damian was the victim, but in a sense, so was I."

"But, Sal," Mike protested. "What if—"

I gave him a push toward the back room. "You must have some calls to make, right? Well, you can do that from the back room." I turned to Josie. "And I'm sure you can find a way to stay busy behind the display case."

Before she could reply, the bells over the front door jingled, and Magnolia walked in. She was dressed in a bright red coat and black leather boots with at least four-inch heels. My swollen feet hurt just looking at them. Mike stood in the doorway of the back room and pretended to be texting on his phone, but his gaze followed us as I gestured to a nearby table.

Magnolia ignored me and went to peer into the display case. "I want some of those gingerbread men."

"Give her two on the house please," I told Josie, who returned Magnolia's sullen stare with a deathlike one of her own.

Without a word, she put two cookies on a plate and handed them to Magnolia. Magnolia crossed back to the table and sat across from me. She took a bite and kept her eyes pinned on Josie, who was standing only a few feet away, arms crossed over her chest.

"You can stop with the bodyguard routine," Magnolia told her. "I'd never hurt anyone. Especially a woman who's preggers."

Josie stared down her nose at Magnolia. "Forgive me if I don't happen to believe you. One false move and I'll have all of Colwestern's police force in here."

"Ah, Jos, don't you have something to do in the back room?" I asked hopefully.

She came and stood behind my chair. "Nope."

I sighed and watched Magnolia gobbling down the gingerbread. "These are fantastic," she said. "Kind of weird how they were found next to Damian's body. He didn't even like gingerbread."

Josie and I exchanged glances. "Did you tell anyone about seeing the cookies at the crime scene?" I asked. "Or only about finding my cake server?"

"The cops asked me to refrain from sharing details about the murder scene. I'll tell you this though. On my way out of the station that night, some weird reporter was waiting for me. He followed me to my car and even offered me fifty bucks if I told him what I'd seen." She bit into her lower lip and stared down at the floor. "I needed the money, so I told him about your knife. But I didn't mention the cookies. Honest."

I gritted my teeth in annoyance. "Cake server." If she said knife one more time, I might stuff that gingerbread man up her nose.

"Sorry," she mumbled.

Well, at least I knew how Jerry Maroon had gotten his information. That man was lower than pond scum. If he hadn't meddled, maybe my shop wouldn't be suffering at its busiest time of year. Instead, he'd spread the news all over his blog. He'd get his just desserts one day, I was certain of it. As Grandma Rosa often said, "Karma was a snitch."

Magnolia's lips quivered. "Your cake server was sticking out of Damian's neck when I found him. There was blood everywhere." She hiccupped back a sob. "It was obvious to me that he was dead. Yeah, I was in shock and didn't know what I was doing, but I remembered seeing your name on the knife…er, server. Then I put two and two together. He'd told me about the carjacking earlier and that you were still hot for him. I guess he was trying to make me jealous, and it worked." Her gaze settled on the doorway to the back room, where Mike was standing, leaning against the frame, his eyes narrowed on her. "Another bodyguard I see. By the way, he's much better looking than he was in high school."

"Finish your conversation," Mike called over. "My wife has more important things to do today."

She glared at him and then addressed me. "Are the cops close to catching Damian's killer?"

Was Magnolia on a fishing expedition? She had both means and motive to have killed her boyfriend. "You should probably talk to them yourself."

"I already told you they won't tell me anything. Besides, I don't trust them." Bitterness filled her voice. "When Farley said you were looking for me, I figured it was a good time to find out what you knew."

"Didn't Dru Ann tell you that I called?" Josie asked.

Magnolia shook her head. "Dru Ann's out of town for her job. She's terrible about returning messages. Farley called last night and said you wanted to see me. He also said he warned you that it wasn't a good idea because I hate your guts." She bit into her lower lip. "I don't hate you. I also don't believe you killed him."

"Any idea who did?" *Or maybe…you?*

A tear rolled down Magnolia's cheek. "No, but whoever did needs to pay. I'll make sure of that."

I tried to look at this from Magnolia's perspective, but it baffled me. "I don't understand. Damian used drugs, sold drugs, cheated on you, and hit you before he turned himself around." I was still doubtful about the last part. "Now, I'm not trying to sound judgmental, but how could you love someone who treated you like garbage?"

"He never hit me," Magnolia said defensively. "Yeah, he had a bad habit, but was trying to clean his act up. Damian hadn't done any drugs since last summer. He was a changed man. It all started when that chick he knew fell overboard."

This caught my attention. "The woman that Farley dated and Rachel was friends with?" It had to figure into Damian's death, but how? "Farley mentioned that his ex died in a boating accident last summer. Were you on the boat too?"

"No." Magnolia sniffed. "Damian was there, but they weren't a couple. Farley dumped her right before the accident because he said she was a total crackhead. She lived in the same apartment building as Damian, which is how Farley met her. He said she was never going to kick the habit."

"Go on," I said quietly.

"A few people saw Damian talking to her right before she fell over the side of the boat. After her body was found, all the passengers were questioned, but they put Damian through the ringer. The pigs were convinced he had something to do with her death but couldn't prove it. He took a couple of lie detector tests and passed them with flying colors. Finally, they decided she must have fallen, and that left Damian in the clear. The tramp had a ton of drugs in her system that day. People on the boat said she couldn't even walk a straight line. If you ask me, she was responsible for her own death."

I wasn't so sure. "What boat are we talking about? The ferry that runs between Rochester and Canada?" I'd never been on it myself but knew they had daily excursions.

"The *Merry Ferry*," Josie said.

Magnolia snapped her fingers. "Yeah, that's the one. I haven't been on it since I was a kid."

Someone else had told me a story about a girl falling into the water, but who? My mind was drawing a blank. I'd read how some women became very forgetful during their pregnancy, and I did feel like I was off my game lately. Damian's murder linked to this woman's death, but how? They'd both been addicts. Had she owed him money and he killed her because of it? Or maybe he'd owed the woman money. As far as I was concerned, this was too much of a coincidence for their deaths not to be linked.

"What if Damian did kill her and someone wanted to get even with him for it?" I pressed. "Maybe Farley?"

"Damian didn't kill her," Magnolia insisted, "and it wasn't Farley. He didn't kill Damian either. He loved him like a brother. It has to be Rachel."

"But you can't be sure," Josie said.

Magnolia glared at her. "Oh, but I am sure. She was jealous of Farley's ex, and she was angry at Damian for getting her hooked on drugs. It all makes sense. Damian may have been on the same boat, but he didn't kill her. There was no motive. Isn't that the term the pigs use?"

"They're cops, not pigs. Maybe she owed Damian money for drugs," I offered.

"Nuh-uh. Damian was too busy scrambling around trying to come up with ways to get his own stash. And he stopped using right after she was killed."

I raised an eyebrow. "You're sure about this?"

"Positive," she answered. "He was looking forward to

getting off parole soon."

If Magnolia was telling me the truth, I was even more confused. If Damian was no longer a drug user, why had someone taken him out? I'd assumed that a jealous girlfriend or ex had it in for him. Or perhaps a dealer for overdue payments. Had I gotten the motive wrong? I'd have to start from scratch, as if I were baking a batch of cookies.

"If Damian wasn't using anymore," I said carefully, "why would he be a marked man? Could it have been a jilted ex-lover? Someone else he was seeing?"

"A bitter girlfriend?" Josie suggested with sarcasm.

Magnolia shot Josie an angry look and rose to her feet. "He wasn't seeing anyone else. I told you, he turned himself around last summer. And I wasn't the one who killed him. Guess it was a mistake to come here." She picked up her coat and marched toward the front door.

"Hang on a second." I struggled to my feet, feeling pressure in my lower belly from the exertion. "Josie didn't mean anything by that. Don't you understand? Everyone who is tied to Damian will be considered a suspect until the real killer is found."

"Yeah, I get that," she huffed. "But I still don't like being referred to as a killer. Look, I've got to run. Thanks for the cookies, but I need to get to work."

"I'm glad you came by," I said. "If you think of anyone else who might have had it in for Damian, will you let me know?"

"Sure." Magnolia placed a hand on the door.

"Wait a second." I took a step toward her. "You never told me the name of the woman who died on the boat."

Suspicion was etched into her face as she turned to face me. "Her name was Tatiana. Tatiana Richards."

The bells over the door jingled with her departure, and at the same moment, alarm bells went off inside my head. Josie and I both stared at each other wide-eyed. *We have a winner.* Tatiana Richards was the woman that Freddie Price was writing about in my father's blog class.

CHAPTER SIXTEEN

"Holy cow." Josie echoed my thoughts. "The woman who died on the boat is the same one your father's student—Freddie—was talking about. And she's Farley's ex-girlfriend. What kind of a coincidence is that?"

"It must relate to Damian's murder," I said.

Mike came over as I pushed the button on my cell for my parents' landline. Dad answered on the second ring. "Hi, baby girl! Is my grandkid on the way yet?"

"No, he's still in the same spot as yesterday. Hey, Dad, do you have a phone number for Freddie Price? I'd like to talk to him about his blog."

My father sounded pleased. "Why don't you come to class next week? You can see everyone's blog firsthand and how they're progressing. Your mom will be helping with editing and could use a second set of eyes to—"

"No," I interrupted. "I need to talk to him now. Can you give me his number? Or ask him to come down to the bakery and bring his laptop with him?"

"Well, I don't know, Sal. I'm a pretty busy guy these days." I could picture my father with his phone in one hand, a genetti in the other, and his chest puffed out with pride. "As a matter of fact, I think I have an agent interested in my next book. Priorities, my girl, priorities."

Good grief. *Another* book? Did the insanity ever end? Gianna and I had hoped that our lives might return to normal. "Dad, that's wonderful, but remember, I am letting you use the upstairs apartment for the class, so maybe you could manage to fit me into your schedule? Or give me Freddie's number, and I'll call him myself."

"Well, that's true enough," my father admitted. "You've been great about the apartment. Next time, leave us all a fortune cookie before class, okay? Only good messages though. It will help keep up my students' momentum. I'll call Freddie and ask him to call you."

"Please do it right away, Dad. This is very important. Thanks."

"Get my grandkid here!" he bellowed into the phone before I clicked off.

Mike placed his hands on my shoulders. "Sal, I've got a customer with a leak in their basement. They swear it's the boiler I installed last month. Personally, I don't think so, but I need to go and check it out. The house is only ten minutes away. We're supposed to get a snowstorm tonight, so they're practically begging me to come by. I promise you no more after this, princess. And I already warned them that if you go into labor, I'm out of there."

I gave him a swift kiss. "It's okay. I'll stay here with Josie for the rest of the afternoon, and she can drive me home."

He gave us both a pensive look. "Are you sure? And who's this Freddie guy you were talking to your father about—he's coming *here*? Is this some other psycho that I need to worry about?"

I laughed. "No, he's one of my dad's students."

Mike arched an eyebrow. "Okay, maybe I *should* be worried then. If he's paying your father good money to teach him how to run some crazy death blog—"

"How long do you think you'll be?" I interrupted.

He shrugged. "Depends how bad the leak is. It shouldn't take more than a few hours though."

"Don't worry. I'll be fine. After we close, I'll have dinner waiting for you."

He kissed me again and tweaked my nose. "I have a feeling you'll be calling me before then. Today's the day. I'm betting on it."

"I hope so." I smiled, then watched him run outside to his truck, blow me a kiss, and zoom off. Mike was floating on cloud nine these days. He was so excited about becoming a father. I was excited too and looking forward to bringing our child into the world with him by my side. After years of dreaming about this moment, it was here. So why was I nervous and scared? It didn't make sense. Damian's killer was still out there, and a strange feeling of foreboding had settled over me. My hands moved protectively to my belly, and I was rewarded with a vibration. *What the*—No, it was my phone beeping from the front pocket of my stretchy maternity pants. "Hello?"

"Hi, Mrs. Donovan? This is Freddie Price from your dad's class. He said you wanted to talk to me."

"Freddie, thanks so much for calling back. Would you have time to stop by my bakery this afternoon? It's about your blog."

"What about it?" he asked, sounding concerned.

"It's nothing bad," I assured him. "I'm curious if you have further information about the woman who fell off the boat last summer, Tatiana Richards? I'm not positive, but I think her death might be related to a man who was murdered the other night."

"You mean that Damian guy? Cool," he breathed into the phone excitedly. "I mean, not cool that he died, of course, but that's, like, really fascinating."

Kids these days. I rolled my eyes at the ceiling.

Freddie prattled on. "I could do a massive story about this with your help. It might even make front page! I know Jerry Maroon would approve."

That name made me want to retch. "Do you have any pictures from the day of the boat accident, or maybe a passenger list?"

"No, I don't have a list. Jerry might know where to get one, but he'd want to know why I—"

I didn't want to go that route. "There must have been camera footage on the boat that day—something to show that Tatiana had contact with Damian, the man who was murdered. You see, he was on the same boat that day, and I'm convinced their deaths are linked somehow. You have pictures that you were going to use on your blog, right? Do you have photos other than crime scene ones?"

"Oh sure," Freddie said. "Jerry lent me some of his."

Good old Jerry to the rescue. "But Jerry's not a

photographer by trade. What was he doing taking pictures that day? Was he a passenger on the boat?"

"No, but he was the first media guy to get there after the accident."

Why was I not surprised? "Tell me what else you know about the boat accident, Freddie."

"Well, Jerry's friend Ben Simms is a professional photographer. He was on board that day with a bridal group who were taking in the excursion before their bachelorette party. The bride-to-be wanted pictures on the water, so she hired Ben for the entire day. After Tatiana went overboard, someone saw her floating in the water and jumped in to save her. They got her back on the boat and headed for the shore, but I think she was already dead. Ben was snapping pictures when a cop saw and confiscated his camera."

I was confused. "Where did the pictures come from then?"

"Since they were digital, he had them backed up to the cloud and still had access to them. Jerry somehow managed to get on board and told me that Ben later gave him copies of the photos. I know Jerry gives him free advertising space in his column sometimes, so it may have been a trade-off."

What a racket that creep was running. "Do you have the photos in your possession?"

"Jerry let me make copies," he replied. "But I should probably tell him that somebody else wants to use them."

I did not want Jerry Maroon involved in the investigation. He'd already done more than enough by making me look like a killer. As far as I was concerned, he was also responsible for the lack of business at the bakery. The guy was a narcissistic jerk who didn't care whom he hurt in order to get his precious story. "Freddie, how about we make our own trade-off?"

"What do you mean, Mrs. Donovan?"

"If you send the pictures to my phone, I promise that I'll give you that exclusive interview you want for your blog." Heaven help me. I'd probably end up a laughingstock of the town, but it was better than people thinking I was a killer.

"Oh wow." He breathed into the phone. "That would be

awesome. I can be home in ten minutes, and then I'll send them after I tell Jerry. He's going to be so proud of me. You know, Jerry told me that I had what it takes to be a reporter like him."

That was too bad. I was certain the kid had morals. "Well, see, that's part of the deal. You can't tell him you sent them to me." Jerry would be all over me like chicken pox. "I promise I won't publish them. I only want to see if there's any photographs of Tatiana and who she might have talked to on the boat."

"But I can't do that." He sounded upset. "Jerry would be furious."

Too bad for Mr. Moron—as my grandmother liked to call him. "I promise you that, if Jerry finds out, I will take the blame and talk to him myself. I have a few things I need to say to him anyway."

"Yes, you do." Josie was standing next to me, listening in.

I put a finger to my lips. "Freddie, you're not going to get into any trouble."

"Well…" He finally relented. "I guess that would be all right. It will take me a few minutes to get home and then sort through them, so give me close to an hour."

"Perfect. Like I said, I'm only interested in ones with people, not the sights. Especially Tatiana and who she might have been with."

"There's a few photos that I haven't looked at yet. Honestly, I'm not sure if Jerry did either. Ben just sent them to Jerry last week when I asked about them for my blog. If you need a close-up photo of Tatiana, I can send you one that ran in the paper the day after her death."

I glanced out the bay window while he was talking and caught the first fluffy white flakes descending from the sky. "Okay, I'll watch for the photos. Thanks for your help, Freddie."

His excited voice rivaled a little kid's. "Man, I'm going to be the talk of the town when I get that interview with you. I mean, you're like a legend in Colwestern."

It was nice that the kid thought I was popular, but he was sorely mistaken. The newspaper hadn't nicknamed my shop Sally's Shambles for nothing. "You've made my day, Freddie," I said and promptly clicked off.

"He's sending the pictures of Tatiana?" Josie asked. She was making sugar cookies in the shape of Christmas trees with miniature-size colorful gumdrops as ornaments. The rich, warm aroma emitting from the oven smelled of vanilla and sugar. Unable to resist, I grabbed a spoon and helped myself to some of the frosting, then smacked my lips together. Creamy, sweet, and strawberry. I glanced down at the tray Josie was working on. It was frosting similar to the icing she'd used on the leftover gingerbread cookies—only this was a thicker texture.

The gingerbread men with strawberry frosting. The cookies that nobody had wanted to buy.

Quickly, I took stock of what I knew about Damian's crime scene. Two gingerbread men had been found next to my cake server and Damian's body. There had been a dozen left in the case the day before the killer broke in and stole my server and cookies. What had happened to the rest of the gingerbread men? Magnolia said that Damian didn't even like gingerbread. Did his killer have a sweet tooth?

I scrunched my eyes shut and tried to think, but my level of concentration was off. There was a detail about the cookies I'd overlooked. What was it?

"You okay?" Josie asked.

"Fine." I washed the spoon and set it in the drying rack.

Josie was watching me intently. "What do you expect to find in the pictures? One of Tatiana talking to Damian? He was cleared by the cops, remember?"

"Yes, I'm aware of that. I'm not sure what I'll find," I said honestly. "Maybe Damian helped kill her—I don't know. Perhaps the so-called Head Elf I texted you about last night was on the boat—the same person who wanted Lyle and Leroy to kill Damian. Think about the scenario. Farley's ex-girlfriend supposedly falls, or was pushed, off a boat. Months later Damian—who'd known her, sold her drugs at one point, and was on the same excursion when she died—is murdered. It seems like a weird coincidence. And remember, Magnolia said that Damian started to clean up his drug act about the same time as the boating accident."

"Farley could have killed Damian," Josie said. "But what

would his motive be? And he broke up with Tatiana—she didn't break up with him. Rachel also dated Damian, remember. Perhaps she did it to get even for the way he treated her. And don't count out Magnolia. Sorry, but I still don't trust her."

"Me either." My back was killing me as I sat down on the stool next to the worktable. "I'd like to go visit Rachel today but don't have the energy."

Josie narrowed her eyes. "If it's not Rachel, Farley, or Magnolia, who else is there that killed Damian?"

I shrugged. "No idea."

A muscle worked on her jawbone. "Sal, is there any chance it could be someone that you helped put behind bars? Think for a moment. Could any of those people have had a connection to Damian, gotten out of jail, and decided to come after you? It happened once before, in case you've forgotten."

No, I hadn't forgotten. Someone had tried to kill me right before my wedding as an act of revenge. I drew my eyebrows together and considered her question. "I don't think so. The only other person might be Lyle, but I don't see how since he was one of my carjackers."

"It was only a thought. I like to consider all the options." She pointed at my belly with the decorating tip in her hand. "You've dropped again, I can tell. Better be careful, girl. It could be any time now."

"Nope. I'm convinced this kid plans to stay in here forever." Not that I could blame him. Why would my poor child want to be subjected to all the craziness in my life? I wouldn't wish that on anyone.

The bells on the door came to life. Josie glanced into the storefront, her face full of hope, and then she frowned. "Oh. It's only Brian."

"Gee, thanks," he called out, sarcasm heavy in his tone. We walked out of the back room together to greet him. He watched me rubbing my back and smiled. "I passed your husband on the road and figured you might be here. Dedicated to the job—up to the very last minute."

Despite his joke, I sensed something was wrong. "Okay, spill it. What's going on?"

"Magnolia came into the station a little while ago," he

said. "She demanded to know more details of Damian's murder and asked why you were privy to his information. What have you been telling her?"

"Oh, for goodness' sake. I didn't tell her anything, Brian. Why would I share information with someone we know is a suspect? Magnolia told me she didn't trust the police and wanted to know what I knew. She's fishing for information. While you're here, I have my own questions."

He folded his arms over his chest. "I'm not promising that I'll answer any but go ahead."

"Do you remember hearing about a woman who fell over the side of the *Merry Ferry* last summer?"

Doubt clouded his bright green eyes. "Why are you asking?"

"Because I believe it may have something to do with Damian's murder." Brian might think I was crazy, but I didn't care. "Damian was on that same boat trip. The woman's name was Tatiana Richards. She was also Farley's ex-girlfriend. A good friend of hers, Rachel Hedley, started dating Farley shortly before Tatiana died."

Brian's face became a brilliant shade of crimson. "Didn't I tell you to leave this alone? Go have your baby, and let us find Damian's killer, Sally. You've been cleared of possible charges, so please stay out of the investigation."

"I'll be in the freezer getting dough if you need me," Josie said and left the room. She'd heard this song and dance from Brian several times before and knew how it was going to end.

"Brian, I've been trying to stay out of it," I protested. "Somehow I keep getting pulled back in."

He sighed. "If you must know, yes, I do remember that case. It sounded pretty fishy to me at the time. I was away that week on vacation but did see photographs when I returned. If I recall correctly, the woman had a lot of drugs in her system, and they concluded she fell over the side. Do you think Damian killed her?"

"Maybe. If not, he might have seen it happen and chosen not to do anything about it. My question is, why was she killed? What was the motive?"

Brian raised his hand. "Hold off on any more investigating for a while. I'm going back to the station to see if I can get access to Tatiana's file. Normally I wouldn't dream of looking into a case that isn't mine, but I have a legit excuse since this may link to another murder. I'll call you if I find out anything."

CHAPTER SEVENTEEN

―――

An hour passed, and there were still no pictures from Freddie. Impatience was my middle name today. Despite the pain in my lower back, I had a sudden burst of energy and decided to whip up a batch of chocolate-filled cookie cups to keep myself occupied.

Josie shook her head. "A true baker right up until delivery," she teased.

"Why hasn't Freddie sent the pictures yet?" I demanded as I placed the mini muffin tins into the oven.

"I don't know. Why do we have no customers?" Josie went into the front room and stared mournfully out the window. "It's almost five, Sal. I don't know if it's worth it to stay open until six."

"I'll stay until the cookie cups finish," I volunteered. "You go ahead. I'm sure I could get my father or grandmother to give me a ride home."

"No way. I'm not going to leave you here alone with a chance of you going into labor," Josie said. "Plus, Mike would kill me. I'm praying for a big avalanche of customers tomorrow. God, we need it. Say, what's going on with Gianna? Is this wedding still happening?"

I shrugged. "I'm always the last one to know anything. My mother tried to phone Gianna earlier, and I texted her as well, but she hasn't responded. It wouldn't surprise me if she took off. Hopefully, with Johnny and the baby," I quickly added. My sister had been under so much pressure between work, wedding, and motherhood that I feared she was going to have a nervous breakdown. My father's insane hearse idea might have pushed her over the edge. Secretly, I hoped that Gianna and Johnny would elope so that I didn't have to waddle down the aisle in a dress that was now large enough to cover the walls of my bedroom.

"Poor thing," Josie said sympathetically. "What about Mike? Is he coming to get you, or are you riding home with me?"

"He texted me a little while ago. The boiler is worse off than he thought. He doesn't think he'll be finished for another couple of hours."

The bakery's landline rang at the same time as Josie's ringtone, which was set to "Santa Claus Is Coming to Town." She stared at me sheepishly. "Sorry. Stupid choice. I should have changed it." She hurried into the kitchen to take her call while I answered the bakery's landline.

"Hey." A deep male voice, slightly familiar, responded to my greeting. "It's Farley. Is this Sally?"

My stomach muscles tightened. I was being silly. Even if Farley had killed Damian, he couldn't hurt me over the phone. "Hi, what's up?"

"Damian's funeral is tomorrow," he said quietly.

"On Christmas Eve?" How depressing.

"Yeah. The funeral home had an opening, so we jumped on it."

I hoped this wasn't an invitation to attend. "You're in charge of the details?"

"He doesn't have any family here," Farley said. "And that's what friends do for one another."

"What about Magnolia? She was his girlfriend."

An ominous silence followed. "Why are you asking me so many questions?"

I didn't know when to quit sometimes. "Sorry, but one more. Why are you calling me?"

"Oh, right. I need some cookies for the shindig after the funeral. You know—the gathering. About six dozen or so. We're not expecting a big crowd."

Gee, it was difficult to imagine why. Instantly I chided myself for my internal snark. *Don't be like that, Sal. The man is dead, after all.* An order was an order, so I grabbed a page from the notepad on the counter. Josie's voice, loud and distressed, drifted in from the back room. "Farley, can you hang on a second?" I put a hand over the phone. "Jos, what's wrong?"

Josie was already putting on her coat. "The baby fell and cut his lip. Rob thinks he's going to need stitches. I need to go and meet them at the emergency room. Do you want to come with me?" Jeremy was almost four, but everyone still regarded him as the baby.

Alarmed, I dropped my phone on the table. "Is he all right?"

She let out a loud sigh as she buttoned her coat. "I think so. Rob's a wreck though. Men! His mother is at home with the boys. I almost wish she'd taken the baby to the hospital instead. God knows I love Rob, but he doesn't have a clue sometimes."

"Okay, okay. It was an accident." I handed Josie her purse. "Everything will be fine."

"Do you want me to drop you home first?" Josie asked.

"No, I'll call my father to come get me after the cookies are done. Plus I've got an order on the phone I need to take. You go. I'll be fine."

She cast me a worried look. "Lock the front door after I leave."

"I will. Now go. I told you I'm all right."

Josie hurried out the back door, and I closed and locked it after her. I walked back to the phone slowly. The pain in my lower back had become worse in the last few minutes. Feeling drained, I sat down on the stool. Maybe I should call my father now. I glanced at the clock. It was after five and doubtful we'd get many more sales. The cookies only needed to bake a few more minutes.

"Sorry about that, Farley."

"Everything okay?" he asked.

"Fine. What kind of cookies would you like?"

"Let's see…one dozen chocolate chip, one dozen of those kind with the strawberry jam in the middle."

"Thumbprint cookies," I said aloud as I wrote.

He coughed into the phone. "Yeah, right. And four dozen gingerbread men."

'Tis the season, even for funerals, I guess. "What time did you want to pick them up?"

"How about in five minutes?" he asked.

Uneasiness swept over me. "Um, no, I'm afraid not. We're closed but open at nine tomorrow. How's that sound?"

Farley paused. "Yeah, I guess that would be all right. Hey, did Magnolia come to see you?"

"Yes, she did." Was he looking for information now too?

"Did she tell you who she thinks killed Damian?"

My phone beeped, and I saw that I had another call coming in. Brian's number flashed across the screen. "Farley, I have to go. We can talk more tomorrow when you come in." Little did Farley know I wouldn't be alone. Josie and Mike would be with me. There would be no taking chances for me.

"Oh, I forgot one thing," Farley said. "All strawberry frosting on the gingerbread dudes. None of the white stuff."

"You mean icing. See you tomorrow." I hurriedly picked up Brian's call. "Hi. Are you still there?"

"Sally, I just pulled the file for Tatiana Richards's death and found some interesting information."

A delayed lightbulb clicked on in my brain. "Oh God," I whispered.

Brian's voice was anxious. "Sally? Is everything okay?"

Farley's words came back to me. "Brian, I think I know who killed Damian and possibly Tatiana too."

"Farley," he said quietly.

"Yes. He just called to order cookies for Damian's service tomorrow. He asked for four dozen gingerbread with strawberry icing. I should have figured it out the other day when he was here. He ate two gingerbread men, but they had vanilla icing, and he was clearly disappointed while he ate them." I wanted to thunk my head against the wall. Who would have thought my cookies would hold the key to the killer's identity? "I should have put it together then."

"Don't beat yourself up. Would you like to know what I discovered from Tatiana's autopsy report?" he asked.

There was only one thing I could think of. "She was pregnant with Farley's child."

"You're close, but no cigar this time," Brian said. "The autopsy showed that she'd had an abortion only days before."

"Oh wow." The pieces in the puzzle had finally all come

together. Either it had been Farley's baby and she hadn't told him, or she'd been sleeping around on him. "How come this information didn't come out sooner? If Jerry Maroon had known, he would have plastered it on all the billboards in Colwestern."

"Tatiana's mother asked that it not be divulged," Brian said. "Since her death was ruled an accident back then, we had no problem consenting to her request."

Another Braxton Hicks hit me, and I winced from the discomfort. "It was no accident, Brian. You and I both know that. Is there any way to identify the father?"

"No. If she'd still been pregnant at the time of the accident, tests could have determined the father. But not this way."

"Damian must have known that Farley killed her. Was Damian blackmailing him? Do you have enough information to arrest Farley?"

"I can bring him in for questioning again," Brian said, "and we'll see where it leads. Unfortunately, that's all I can do for now. Where are you?"

"I'm at the bakery, ready to close up."

Brian cleared his throat. "Don't go near this guy, Sally. I mean it. Call him back and tell him to get his cookies elsewhere."

The wheels began to turn inside my head. "Maybe we could try to trap him. He's coming in tomorrow morning for his order. What if you waited on him instead of me?"

To my surprise, Brian seemed to be considering the idea. "Let me see if I can track him down tonight. If not, that's a possibility. Now close up the shop and go home." His radio sounded in the background. "I need to respond to this call. Talk to you later."

My phone's battery had a 2 percent charge left, so I plugged my charger into the wall and left it on the wooden block table before dialing my parents' landline. No one answered. That was strange. I left a message and asked them to call me back when they got home. I'd wait a few minutes, and if they didn't respond, I'd phone Mike.

I removed both trays of cookies from the oven and set them in the metal rack. They smelled wonderful. The aroma of chocolate was soothing when I didn't feel my best. I was afraid I'd overdone it today and walked slowly into the front room. Darkness had settled over the town, and the snow was coming down at a furious pace. As I started toward the front door to lock it, the baby gave a hard, sharp kick that left me breathless and winded. I had to sit down in a chair, and I grabbed the back of another one for support while gritting my teeth through the pain. This didn't feel like the false ones I'd been having for days. As I tried to gain my strength back enough to stand, a shadow passed in front of the window, and I panicked. The bells rang before I could even rise out of the chair.

Farley waved at me and moved over to the bakery case, both his hands shoved deep in his pockets. His gray eyes were cold and aloof and sent a chill through me.

"Sally, I came for my order."

Terror seized me as I clung to the chair. "Sorry, Farley. We're closed. It's not ready yet anyway."

He chuckled in a low, menacing undertone that formed icicles between my shoulder blades. "I'm sure you can find me something. Don't worry. I've got plenty of time to kill."

CHAPTER EIGHTEEN

———

If I hadn't been in such pain already, I would have tried to kick myself. I wouldn't be in this predicament if I'd gotten to the door sooner. Help was only a phone call away, so I reached into my stretchy pants pocket for my phone. *My phone!* I'd left it to charge on the backroom table. *Okay, maybe we're wrong. Maybe he's not the killer.* Freddie hadn't sent the pictures yet, so they might reveal something different.

"You didn't tell me what Magnolia had to say," he said.

Somehow, I had to make it into the back room without him following me. I tried to act casual. "Oh, she wanted to know if the police had information, but they didn't tell me anything. They never do. I told her what happened with Leroy and Lyle. You heard about that, right?"

He waved a hand dismissively. "Yeah. That's old news." His eyes traveled to the bakery case. "Oh, you've got my favorites." He pointed to the Christmas tree cookies Josie had frosted before she left.

"Would you like one?"

He licked his lips in anticipation. "I'll take six. Man, they look good. Much better than those gingerbread cookies you gave me last time."

This confirmed my earlier suspicion. I was positive Farley was the one who'd killed Damian, and I tried to remain calm. "You like strawberry, huh?"

Farley's eyes, cold and devoid of emotion, searched mine. A shiver went down my spine, and the baby gave another sharp kick that had me dropping the waxed paper and clutching my belly in pain.

"You okay?" Farley asked, his voice deadpanned. "And

yeah, I love strawberry. Guess it's kind of an addiction."

Shaking, I reached for a piece of waxed paper and somehow managed to place the six cookies in the bag. I leaned against the case for support. "The baby's active today." I handed the cookies to him. "Do you have any kids?"

His mouth twisted into an ugly expression, and I winced at my unfortunate choice of words. *Stupid, stupid, Sal.* In my defense, I was in so much pain that I could barely stand or think straight.

He ignored my question. "How much for the cookies?" His voice was so low that I could barely make out the words.

I swallowed hard. "Six dollars. You can leave the money on the counter. I'm not feeling well. Good night." I turned and managed to make it into the back room, but I still felt those eyes on me, burning a hole through my skin. The bells jingled, and I breathed a long sigh of relief. Thank God. Farley had gone, and he didn't think I'd suspected him. Somehow, I'd managed to pull it off. Another contraction hit me, and my knees buckled. Oh no. It looked like my time might have finally come. If this was what labor was going to be like, then knock me out right now.

The contraction passed but left me feeling weak and out of sorts. Breathing heavily, I grabbed my phone to call Mike and saw that Freddie had sent the pictures. Distracted, I thumbed through them quickly. The first one was a close-up of Tatiana. It must have been the photo that ran in the paper after her death. She had been a striking girl with long, shiny black hair and green eyes that resembled jewels. The next picture was of her on the boat, the water serving as a backdrop. The difference between the two shots was disturbing. In the later one, Tatiana's hair had dulled, her skin was a sallow-looking color, and her bloodshot eyes appeared dazed.

The next photo showed Damian standing across from her on the boat, and they seemed involved in conversation. The last shot must have been of the bridal party that Freddie had mentioned. A group of women were dancing, and Tatiana was talking to one of them. In the background, Damian was sitting at a table, his eyes pinned on her. A man in a hooded sweatshirt was sitting next to him. I enlarged the picture on my phone for a better look. The man's head was bent forward, and he was holding a cell phone in front of him, but it looked like Farley. I started to send the picture to Brian, when a step sounded behind me. A chill went down my spine.

"Nice shots, huh?"

I gasped. Farley was still here, and he'd seen the photos. I tried to place the phone back in my pocket, but he grabbed my wrist so tightly that I cried out in pain. He studied the screen, and then it went black. "Damn it," he growled. "Don't you know how to keep a phone charged? What were you planning to do with those pictures?"

"Nothing," I whispered.

Farley swore and then pushed me to the floor. I tried to grab the leg of the table to break my fall but missed and went down in a heap on my backside, groaning with pain. Another contraction immediately began and left me immobilized. He pulled out a knife from his pocket, and I whimpered. "No. Please don't.'

He ignored me and opened the back door into the alley, looked both ways, and then slammed it shut. The knife's silver blade glinted under the bright ceiling lights. "Don't worry. I already locked the front door, so we won't be disturbed. Now get up," he ordered me.

"I can't," I moaned. "I think I'm—"

Impatience seeped into every inch of Farley's face. He muttered an expletive, reached down, and yanked me roughly to my feet. I was so dizzy that I almost fell over, but he held tightly to my arm. Sweat ran down the small of my back. "Please don't hurt me," I begged. "Think about my baby."

His face was so close to mine that I could smell the frosting on his breath. "You aren't giving me much choice here, Sally. You know the truth. It's written all over your face."

"I don't know anything," I lied. "Why don't you go ahead and leave, and I'll act like this didn't happen. Leave me and my baby alone, and I'll never say a word. Honest."

"You shouldn't have been snooping around," he snarled and held the tip of the blade near my chin. He looked directly into my eyes, but I sensed he saw someone else. "Tatiana shouldn't have lied to me. She didn't give me a choice." He moved his face away from mine. "One of your cop friends came to the car wash today. When he asked about the boat accident and Tatiana, I knew they were on to me, and I figured you had to be involved too."

Brian hadn't told me he was planning to stop at the car wash. Not that it mattered anymore. I had more important things to think about, like figuring out how to keep myself and my baby alive. Farley kept one arm wrapped around my throat and placed the knife's blade under my chin. My head was spinning, and my legs were so weak I couldn't walk. I had to try to stall until help arrived. Had my father tried calling me back? Mike must have called again by now, but there was no way of knowing since my phone was dead.

"Lyle and Leroy were friends of yours?" I managed to choke out.

Farley snorted. "I never should have trusted those two losers. We all hung out together for years. I thought they were trustworthy—and that Lyle had some kind of brain. Nope, they managed to screw everything up. And I never told them to carjack anyone! They claimed that their car stalled and they spotted you at a traffic light. They figured you'd be an easy target. After they held up the jewelry store and called to tell me, I told them to ditch your car." The knife in his hand shook against my skin. "You want something done right, gotta do it yourself. Know what I mean?"

Fear lodged in my throat, and my voice was hoarse. "You killed Damian because he knew about what happened to Tatiana, di…didn't you? You pushed her over the side of the boat, and he saw you."

An ominous silence filled the room. To my surprise, his grip on me released slightly. He moved the knife away from my throat, but it wasn't enough for me to make a run for it. I clutched the side of the table with one hand, and he made no attempt to stop me. His gaze met mine, and the expression in his eyes changed—to one of sadness.

"I did care about her," he said after a beat. "Tatiana was a major addict though. No matter what you might think, she was hooked before we even met. Then she quickly got worse. She couldn't hold a job, turned her back on her family, and wouldn't get help. She kept hounding me for freebies, and finally, I couldn't take it anymore. I told her we were done."

"It was your baby she was carrying?"

In a fit of sudden rage, he stabbed the worktable with his knife, and I jumped. Okay, wrong thing to say. I had to get out of here, but how? I couldn't even walk. Having a baby in the presence of a killer was going to be far worse than having it at Gianna's wedding.

"She wasn't even going to tell me about the baby," Farley said between clenched teeth. "She slipped and mentioned it to Damian. By the time I confronted her, it was too late. She'd already had an abortion." His face turned the color of a flame. "I had a right to know. That was my kid."

"Of course," I said in my best sympathetic tone.

Farley seemed to be lost in his own little world. "Damian agreed to help me get rid of her, but afterward, I knew he regretted it. I thought he'd start asking for some of my stash to keep quiet, but he stopped using altogether. Instead, he asked for cash to keep mum. At first it was only a few bucks here or there, but when he saw the money I was making off of Leroy and Lyle, he started asking for more. I was planning to leave the country when I had enough saved, and he ruined my plans."

"So you had to kill him."

"He kept threatening to squeal until I couldn't stand it anymore," Farley said. "The night that he mentioned running into you, everything fell into place perfectly. Now someone else had a motive to kill him. When I came here and saw the alarm wasn't on, I knew it was fate." He chuckled under his breath.

I doubled over in pain. "Can I sit down on the floor for a—"

He interrupted me, lost in his own thoughts. "Lyle and Leroy were like my own robots. They did what I said, no questions asked. They seemed happy with the money they were earning, but that damned Damian was just too greedy. Lyle and Leroy told me that they killed a guy before. I believed them, but they must have lied. So, I told Leroy to kill Damian." Farley seemed to come out of his trance. He grabbed my arm and pushed me away from the table. "Are you listening to me?"

"Yes." My legs were giving out under me. "Please let me sit down."

He let go of me, and I thankfully slid to the floor, clutching my belly. I had to get to a hospital, but there wasn't much chance of that. No one even knew I was in trouble. Mike thought I was comfortable at home by now. Josie assumed that my father had picked me up. After weeks of people hovering over me, not allowing me to breathe by myself, the irony of the situation did not escape me. My time had finally come, and no one was here to help me except for a cold-blooded killer. A classic Sally moment.

Farley seemed oblivious to my pain and distress. "And what did they do? They chickened out on me at the last second. I had no choice but to get rid of Damian myself."

"Weren't you afraid that Lyle and Leroy would tell people you had killed Damian?"

Farley laughed again. "You did meet them, right? Nah, I wasn't worried. Damian had a lot of enemies. He owed people money. Those two clowns were the biggest saps ever born. It's a shame that you had to find Damian's address in your car though, thanks to those two idiots. Can you believe I even had to write down the freaking address because they couldn't remember it?" He shook his head ruefully. "It's so hard to find good help these days, ya know?"

"Totally," I choked out as I stared up at him. Farley was fingering the blade of the knife thoughtfully. If I only had something to stab him in the leg with. I glanced around me and spotted a fork under the stove a few feet away. I inched backward slightly. He didn't seem to notice.

"How could Tatiana do that to me?" Farley's voice shook with rage. "She should have told me. She killed my baby, so she didn't deserve to live either."

"I'm sorry." I tried to sound grief-stricken for him, but it was difficult, given what he had done to Tatiana. The entire scenario sickened me. One thing I had learned a long time ago—never try to argue with a psychopath. There was no winning. I slid backward on the floor a couple of more inches. The fork was almost within reach. I stretched out my hand behind my back, praying he wouldn't see.

Farley's jaw tightened. "I know what's going on in your mind. You're trying to think of how to get away from me. Forget it, Sally. There *is* no way. Your life is over."

Panic surged through me and mixed with nausea. I tried to remain calm. "You went to a lot of trouble to pin Damian's death on me."

"Not really," Farley said. "He was costing me money, and I needed it to stop. I used my picks to break into the bakery, and with no alarm to worry about, it was a piece of cake. Or cookie. Ha-ha, get it? Then I spotted that cake thingy with your name on it. So, it really wasn't trouble until you started sticking your fat nose into everything."

My hand closed around the fork as Farley saw it. He jumped forward and smacked it out from under my hand. I grabbed him around the leg, and he kicked me in the chest, leaving me winded. I cried out in pain, and my back connected with the hard tiled floor.

"Get up," he growled, but I couldn't move.

Spots danced before my eyes, and I struggled not to pass out. If I did, I was a goner for sure.

Farley muttered another swear word and lifted me roughly to my feet. I stumbled against him. "You're done asking questions," he hissed. "You did this all to yourself. Time to go now."

He was shoving me toward the back door. The room began to spin. I clutched at the doorway and tried to catch my breath. "Why don't you just drop me off at the hospital on your way to Mexico, okay?"

Farley shook his head sadly. "Sorry, but I can't let you live. You'd go to the cops. I'm gonna have to kill you, and put you in the trunk, then dump your body somewhere. Now move it."

"I can't—" I gasped. It was too difficult for me to move. "Please. I think I'm going to faint."

"Stop stalling. I told you to move it!"

He gave me another shove, and I stumbled against the door. "I'm in labor."

Farley laughed as he opened the back door. "That bites."

The pressure on my bladder was so intense that I couldn't bear it any longer. A trickle of water ran down my leg. "Oh God," I breathed. "I really *am* in labor."

Farley's eyes were large and terrified as he stared at the small puddle on the floor and swore. "You've got to be kidding me! Why does this stuff always happen to me? Well, it just means I'll have to kill you quicker." He started to pry my hands from the doorway.

"No!" I sobbed. "Think about my baby. What about your baby, the one who never got to live? Do you really want to see that happen to another innocent child?"

Farley's face froze into immobility for a moment, and then he instantly recovered and tried to drag me out of the kitchen. "Sorry, Sally. I don't have a choice."

As he tried to push me, I caught sight of the rolling pin in the dish drainer a couple of feet away. There was no way to reach it. He caught my eyes moving around the room and gave me another push. I stumbled and almost fell. From the doorway, I stared down at the pavement in the alley and spotted a pair of black boots. Maybe I was hallucinating.

"Who the hell are you?" Farley barked from behind me.

I looked up and found myself staring at an elderly man with a shock of white hair. He was wearing a red bomber jacket and a Santa hat. "Nick," I choked out. It was the same man who'd helped me after the carjacking.

Somehow, I managed to get to my feet as Farley pointed the knife at him. "Get out of my way, old man, unless you want to die too."

Nick folded his arms across his chest. "I hope you're taking Sally to a hospital. It's obvious that she's in labor."

Farley took a step toward Nick while I groped backward, feeling for the rolling pin.

"I said to get out of my way, old man. You're no match for me."

Nick roared with laughter. "That's what you think, hotshot. You don't know anything about me."

"Who *are* you?" Farley asked again, and I thought I detected a note of fear in his voice this time.

He took another menacing step toward Nick while I brought the rolling pin down on his head as hard as I could muster. Farley dropped the knife and staggered backward. Nick gave him a shove, and he fell into my cookie rack. The rack and

Farley went down in a heap with an ear-splitting crash.

Nick glanced around the kitchen. "Sally, do you have anything to tie him up with?"

I clutched at my belly, gasping for breath. "Do you have a phone? I need to call for help. You could use his knife to cut the ties off the aprons hanging on the wall. They should be strong enough to hold him."

"Got it," Nick said cheerfully as he handed me his phone. "Are you okay? You look kind of green. Now, that's not a bad color for this time of year, but—"

"Fine," I rasped and typed three familiar digits into the phone. I leaned back against the wall, afraid I wouldn't be able to get back up again. I gritted my teeth through another contraction as an operator came on the line.

"9-1-1. What is your emergency?"

It was a few seconds before I could answer.

"Hello? What is your emergency?"

"Please help," I gasped. "I…uh, have two…two emergencies."

There was silence for a second. "Your location is coming through as 13 Carson Way. What is your name, ma'am, and what are your emergencies?"

"My name is Sally Donovan. A man came into my bakery and he tried to kill me." My forehead was bathed in sweat, and I panted like a dog.

"Where is he now?" The operator's voice sounded puzzled, as if she was trying to get a grip on what had happened. To tell the truth, I wasn't exactly sure what had happened myself.

"I knocked him out with a rolling pin. Please send two ambulances right away."

"Two ambulances?" The operator asked in surprise.

I gritted my teeth, resigned to the fact that I was about to give birth on the bakery's kitchen floor. "The other one's for me. I'm in labor."

CHAPTER NINETEEN

———

The next few hours were a complete blur as I drifted in and out of consciousness. After phoning for help, the next thing I remembered was the sound of wailing sirens and a flash of bright red and blue lights in my face as I was being loaded into an ambulance. I thought Brian was talking to me at some point, but it may have been my imagination. Someone was holding my hand—*Nick?* No, it was Mike. The pain in my lower back was so excruciating that I wanted to weep.

"We've given her something to help her relax." A woman's subdued voice floated through the air. "It's making her very drowsy, but she was hysterical when we found her. It may be a tough delivery for her, Mr. Donovan. That's a big baby she's carrying."

"Are either of them in any danger?" Mike asked anxiously.

I must have drifted off again because the next thing I remembered was a nurse helping me into a hospital gown. I was so weak that I could barely lift my arms. The sides of the bed were lifted and then I was being pushed down a hallway that seemed to have no end. My eyelids fluttered shut again.

When I opened them, Dr. Chandler was in front of my bed, a nurse beside him. Mike was wearing blue scrubs and standing next to me, holding tightly to my right hand. "It won't be long now, princess. Our baby will be here soon."

An hour later, Mike was still saying the same encouraging words. I was bathed in sweat and exhausted. "Can I go home now?" I cried out, and everyone laughed.

"Come on, Sally. Try pushing again." Dr. Chandler's deep voice resonated through the delivery room.

I bore down and gritted my teeth, squeezing Mike's hand so hard that his flesh turned a lifeless white. The doctor's face was unreadable, but the nurse clucked her tongue loudly and shook her head. "Nope. That baby must really like it in there." She laughed, trying to make a joke, but I was not in the mood.

"Come on, Sally. One more time," Dr. Chandler coaxed, and I wanted to burst into tears.

Mike pursed his lips. "Doc, I don't mean to tell you your business, but she's been pushing for over an hour. My wife is tough, but it's plain to see she's exhausted."

"Can I have some water?" My throat was parched, and the dry air in the room wasn't helping.

The nurse shook her head. "Not now."

Mike surveyed her coldly. "What harm is a few ice chips going to do?"

"Let her have them." Dr. Chandler said to the nurse, who immediately held out a blue plastic cup and spoon to Mike. The doctor then spoke to another nurse in an undertone and walked out of the delivery room.

"Why is he leaving?" I shrieked, my mouth full of ice chips. "That's it. He's given up. Our baby's not coming out."

Mike's mouth turned up at the corners, but he was smart enough not to laugh out loud. He kissed me on the cheek and then wiped my sweaty forehead with a cool, wet towel the nurse had handed him. "There's nothing to worry about, sweetheart. The doctor said you need to have a C-section. Our baby's a little too big for you to push out on your own."

With a sigh of relief, I nodded and closed my eyes. I'd wanted a natural delivery—it was all I'd talked about for months. Now, exhausted and weak, I couldn't care less. There was no way I could push anymore. "As long as the baby's okay. That's all that matters."

When he bent over me, I noticed the lines of worry creasing his forehead, but he smiled tenderly into my eyes. "Everything is going to be fine. You rest and let the doctor do all the work. You did a wonderful job, and I'm so proud of you, Sal. You just need a little help, that's all."

My eyes were intent on his face. "Our lives are going to change forever tonight."

He nodded solemnly. "I know, but only for the better. God, Sal, you gave me such a scare when Brian called and said you were in labor. What if that psycho had—" He didn't finish the sentence. "You're one tough cookie. And so's our baby. Get it?" He smiled, obviously pleased with his joke.

"That's cute," I said wearily. So, Brian had been there. Was he in the waiting room with my family? And what about my helpful friend? I stared up at Mike again. "Where's Nick?"

Mike frowned. "Who's Nick?"

"You know." I watched as Dr. Chandler reappeared through the swinging double doors followed by a blond-haired man in a mask and gown. Nurse Anti–Ice Chip flipped a switch on the wall, and the overhead lights became so bright that I had to shield my eyes against them. "I told you. He's the guy who found me when I was carjacked."

The man in the gown came over and patted me on the arm. "Hi, Sally. I'm Dr. Wilson, the anesthesiologist. I'll be giving you an epidural, and then we'll get this show on the road, okay?"

"Thanks, Doc." Mike turned back to me, a perplexed look on his face. "Sal, you were alone when the EMTs got there. Well, except for Farley, whom you'd managed to knock out with the rolling pin. Brian heard the emergency call come in and got to the bakery as soon as the EMTs did. You passed out before they even loaded you into the ambulance, and he called me right away. There was no one else there. You must have been dreaming."

"No," I insisted. "He was there. I *know* he was there."

Mike's midnight blue eyes were anxious. "Okay, princess. I'm sure he was. Don't get yourself upset, okay? You can ask Brian about it tomorrow. He said he'll stop by in the morning to see you."

"What time is it?" I asked groggily.

Mike glanced across the room. "It's 11:50."

"At night?" I asked stupidly.

"Yes." He kissed me lightly on the lips. "Almost Christmas Eve."

Dr. Chandler's voice was warm and soothing. "Okay, Sally, the epidural should have taken effect by now. We're going to transfer you to the operating room, so lay back and enjoy the ride."

Great. Everyone was a comedian these days.

The doctor went on. "Mike, you'll need a mask for the surgery. Angela, get him one please."

Within seconds I was being wheeled into the operating room. Mike gripped me tightly by the hand and only left me for one brief moment to put his mask on. The other nurse hung a sterile blue drape in front of me so that I wouldn't be able to see the surgery. I must have dozed off again for a minute because Mike was squeezing my hand, saying, "Did you hear him, princess? The doctor said our baby will be here in a minute."

There was no more pain, and I smiled up at my husband in a foggy haze. I was tired but didn't want to miss the moment when my child came into the world. My crazy delivery room dream came back to me, and I glanced around the room, afraid I might see my mother with a video camera. "There's no one else with Dr. Chandler except the nurses, right?"

Mike chuckled. "Who did you expect? The stork?"

"It's—complicated." The nurse and Dr. Chandler were talking in hushed voices. There was a tugging sensation on my lower abdomen, and then I heard a cry. It was the most beautiful sound I'd ever heard. I clutched Mike's hand tightly. "Can you see him? Our baby? Is he okay?"

The curtain lowered, and Mike smiled down at me, his eyes moist. "I was right."

"About what?"

"It's a girl, sweetheart."

Tears dripped down my cheeks. "We have a daughter."

"A healthy, beautiful baby girl. Let's get a weight on her and clean her up, and then she's all yours," Angela called out. A few seconds later, I heard her say, "Ten pounds, two ounces. Time of birth, 12:03 a.m., December 24th."

"Way to go, Sally." Dr. Chandler stripped off his gloves and smiled at both of us. "That's the biggest baby born here this month, I believe."

Angela carried my baby to me and placed the warm bundle in my arms. She was wrapped in a white blanket, a pink knit cap sitting on her tiny head covered with dark hair. I stared down at her in wonder, with Mike's arm around my shoulders. Her eyes were enormous and a milky shade of blue. They were transfixed on the bright lights above. I knew the color might change, but I prayed she'd have her father's eyes—the most incredible eyes in the world.

"She's so beautiful," I whispered.

Mike reached out a finger to touch her hand. "She's a wonder, princess. As pretty as her mother." He leaned down to kiss her and me.

I kissed my baby on the forehead and held her out to Mike. "I'm so tired that I'm afraid I might drop her. She's heavy! You take her."

His grin stretched from ear to ear as he held his daughter. He seemed to be a natural at fatherhood already, his hand supporting the back of the baby's head as he cradled her against his chest. The baby looked at him and then closed her eyes, as if content to sleep. "She knows she's in a good place," I said tenderly.

Mike's eyes filled with tears as he held her. I'd only seen him cry a handful of times, and the sight tugged at my heart. "We're all in a good place now, Sal. The three of us are a family—a bond that will never be broken." His voice was gruff with emotion, and his megawatt smile brighter than all the lights in the room. "This is the happiest day of my life."

"Mine too." I smiled up at him.

* * *

Mike lay next to me in a cot the hospital had brought for him. We didn't sleep much, although the baby did. We were too busy counting toes and fingers and trying to decide who she looked like. If her eyes stayed blue, she'd be a carbon copy of her father, except for the nose. That distinct feature belonged to the Muccios.

I'd been worried the baby might have issues nursing, but she'd latched on immediately with no problems. She was already too big for the newborn diapers the hospital provided. Several of the outfits I received at my shower last month wouldn't fit her either, but I didn't care. Because of her size, the nurse said she might start off sleeping three to four hours between feedings. As tired as I was, that made me happy. I wanted to spend every waking moment with her and Mike and never waste another minute.

We had so much to look forward to. Her first smile, learning to walk and talk, riding a bike, birthday parties, graduation, and someday her wedding. I was a regular waterfall just thinking about it all.

My parents had been in briefly after the delivery, but since it was so late, Grandma Rosa had convinced them to come back in the morning. "Sally and her little family need to rest." She'd patted my cheek, and her solemn brown eyes had been moist. "You love hearing that, *cara mia*. And you deserve to hear it. Your face is lit up like a Christmas tree. You have waited a long time for this. Enjoy every minute, sweet girl."

"But has she got a name yet?" my mother called out as my grandmother ushered her out of the room.

Grandma Rosa winked as she shut the door behind them. "I am sure that Sally and Mike will come up with the perfect name for their beautiful baby."

Mike changed the baby and rocked her in his arms, talking to her in a soft voice. I loved watching him with her. He glanced over at me and smiled. "How do you feel about another one, princess?"

"Not tonight," I teased. "I've got a headache."

He yawned, then placed the baby in her plastic bassinet. She let out a little cry as he swaddled her in the blanket like the nurse had shown us earlier. He pointed at the sign on the bassinet that read *I'm a girl!* with *Baby Donovan* written underneath. "She still needs a name, and I think—no, I *know* that I've got it covered."

"Oh yeah?" The pain from my incision was starting to recede. The nurse had given me morphine a little while ago and assured me it wouldn't hurt the baby. I was starting to feel the drug's effects as I yawned and clasped Mike's hand. "How about Michele? It's close to Michael."

He grinned and stroked my hair softly. "Nope. Not a chance. Now you need to get some rest, Mrs. Donovan. We'll talk about it later."

CHAPTER TWENTY

———

"Sal, if you weren't in the hospital right now, I would be screaming for you to get in here. There's a line out the front door!" Josie said excitedly.

"Maybe Grandma would be willing to stop by." My gaze focused on the elderly woman sitting next to my bed as we spoke.

"No, it's fine," Josie assured me. "Mickey's here to help, and Dodie's…well, coping. As soon as we close, I'm on my way over to see that gorgeous little girl. Say, what about the wedding tonight? I brought my dress here so that I could change since I won't have time to go home. But there's no way you can be her matron of honor now! What—"

"Whoa, slow down." I glanced over at Gianna and Johnny, who were sitting on the other side of my bed. Alex was on Johnny's lap, drinking a bottle. Mike handed our baby to Gianna, and she cooed over her as Mike snapped photos with his phone. "As for Gianna's wedding, it's over."

"What?" Josie sounded confused. "Did they call it off because of Satan's clone—aka Nicoletta?"

"No. They went to the courthouse yesterday and made it official."

Josie sucked in some air. "Good for them. How is your mother taking it?"

"Surprisingly well." Gianna and I exchanged a knowing smile. "She and my father are due here any minute. Gianna and Johnny are here with Grandma. Nicoletta, well, that's another story. She's sulking, but she'll get over it."

"In about a hundred years," Johnny said wryly.

I paused for a sip of apple juice left over from my

breakfast tray. "They're planning a small party on New Year's Eve to celebrate the wedding after I'm up and around. Of course, you and Rob are invited. It will be at Kung Foo Parlor."

"Shut up." Josie laughed. "A Chinese restaurant? What did the old lady have to say about that?"

"Johnny told her she could bring her own spaghetti if she wanted."

Josie snorted. "That must have gone over well. Well, if they need extra fortune cookies, we've got it covered. What's happening with psycho Farley?"

I paused to watch Johnny lift Alex next to the baby. He let him touch her black silky hair for a brief second.

"This is your cousin," Gianna told him gently.

The sight of them together pulled at my heart strings. How wonderful that they would always have each other to play with, much like Gianna and me.

"Sal?" Josie called. "You still there?"

"Sorry. Farley admitted to pushing Tatiana overboard and stabbing Damian. Brian sent me a text earlier. He's going to stop by later and fill me in further after he's questioned him."

"One less nutcase that the world has to worry about," Josie remarked. "It's kind of disturbing how they always manage to find you. Sal, you must have a guardian angel looking out for you."

I laughed but didn't mention Nick again. Everyone seemed to think he was some figment of my hormone-crazed imagination, but I knew that wasn't the case. And Josie was one of the biggest skeptics around when it came to ghosts, spirits, or fortune cookie messages.

"You did really good, partner," Josie said. "A ten-pound baby—holy cow! None of mine even came close to that weight. It might have killed me. I can't wait to see the little love."

"She's not so little." I laughed. "She weighs a ton."

"It must be all that cheesecake you ate during your pregnancy," Josie teased. "Give her a kiss from her Aunt Josie. I'll stop by later with a present for her. I wanted to get out of here early to see you but not sure that's going to happen."

"No! Don't leave early. It's Christmas Eve, and we need the money. I'm not going anywhere for a couple of days. How's

Dodie doing?"

Josie sighed. "Still clumsy. But what can I say? It's Christmas. I'm full of holiday cheer today and haven't lost my temper—yet."

"For you, that's a major milestone," I chuckled.

"Oh, we're getting buried here. Gotta run, Sal. Love ya."

I clicked off. Perhaps Dodie wasn't so bad after all. I was looking at the world through rose-colored glasses today. Maybe we should keep her on part time for a while. I was going to need help, and she worked cheaply enough that her talent would eventually surpass the money she cost us in damages. At least I hoped so.

A tap sounded on my door, and my mother poked her head in. "Hi, honey." When she spotted Gianna holding the baby, she squealed.

"Mother!" Gianna spoke indignantly in her sophisticated attorney voice. "People are trying to rest here. Remember, it *is* a hospital."

My mother seemed to have forgotten my father was behind her and almost slammed the door in his face. "Let me see that little sweetie!" She held out her arms for the baby, and Gianna gently laid the baby in them.

My mother crossed the room with the baby, gave Mike and me each a kiss, and then sat down in Gianna's discarded chair and began to cry. "She's so beautiful!"

My father's chest was puffed out with pride as he shook Mike's hand and then leaned down to give me a kiss on the cheek. "You did real good, baby girl. She's a beauty." He smiled slyly at Mike. "Sorry, son. She looks Sicilian."

"No, she doesn't," Gianna scoffed. "She looks just like her father."

My father pretended not to hear. "Yep. A true-blue Italian. Except those eyes. But they'll turn dark in a few weeks."

Mike bit into his lower lip to keep from laughing, while Grandma Rosa shook a finger in my father's face. "I have a feeling they are going to stay the same color. Not every grandchild of yours must look Italian, *pazza*."

"Okay, okay." My father held up a hand. "I'm just glad that she and her mother are all right." His expression turned solemn as he stared at me. "You've had too many close calls, baby girl. You've got to be more careful from now on, okay? There's a little person who needs you—more than anything."

His words both touched and surprised me. I raised an eyebrow at Mike, and he looked as amazed as me. My father never waxed philosophical unless he was talking about his beloved blog.

"But what's her name?" Mom asked. "You have decided on one, right?"

I glanced over at Mike, who was grinning broadly at me. "Yes, Mike came up with it. It's perfect for her."

My mother gave me an impatient look. "Well, are you going to share it with us?"

"Tell them, sweetheart," I said to my husband.

Mike squeezed my hand and looked over at the baby, sleeping peacefully in my mother's arms. "We're going to call her Corinne. Corinne Isabella."

Gianna clapped her hands. "Corinne Isabella Donovan. Grandma's middle name and Sal's. That's perfect, Mike."

"It *is* nice." My mother sounded sulky. "Of course, Maria is a nice name too."

My grandmother smiled with pleasure. "That is very thoughtful, my dears. Thank you. But that is a big name for such a little baby. Perhaps she should have a nickname."

Mike winked. "Well, we thought of that too, Rosa. We have the perfect name for our tough little girl. Cookie." He leaned down to kiss me. "If Sal hadn't come back home to start her own cookie shop, we might never have gotten back together. And we may never have had this precious gift. She's a tough cookie, just like her mother. Last night proved that."

Gianna's face lit up. "I love it."

"Cookies are one of my favorite things," my father mused. "Especially the ones that Josie makes. Unless you want to name her Fortune and have her middle name be Cookie."

I shuddered. "No, Dad. Enough with the fortune cookies. They're a moneymaker for the bakery. That's all. There's nothing to them."

Mike looked impressed. "Well, hallelujah. I'm so glad to hear you say that, princess. It's only taken, what—three years?"

"Cookie is a cute name," my mother admitted. "Almost as nice as Maria."

My grandmother nodded approval as my mother handed her the baby. "It is a beautiful name for a beautiful baby. She even smells a little bit like vanilla."

"That's my shampoo." Gianna laughed. "It really is the perfect name for her."

My mother turned to look at Gianna, hurt registering on her lovely face. "Darling, I know you were trying to consider Sal's condition, but I still wish you'd gone through with the wedding. All of your relatives were so disappointed."

Gianna opened her mouth to speak, but Johnny interrupted. "I'm sorry, Maria, but it was our decision. We wanted to get married without all the fanfare. Everything quickly got out of hand thanks, in part, to my grandmother. I'm sorry that you were disappointed." He lifted Alex in his arms and leaned down to give Gianna a kiss. "We're happy, and that's what matters."

"Well." My mother sighed. "That's true enough. And you are having a reception next week." Her face brightened. "I just love a party. Especially on New Year's!"

"Your entire life is a party," my grandmother reminded her.

"Sal, I'm sorry." Gianna's lower lip trembled. "It was selfish of me to plan a wedding for the same week you were expecting. You were such a good sport about it too."

"It wasn't a big deal," I assured her. "Like your husband said, you're married and you're happy, which is what counts."

Mom leaned over the bed to kiss me again. "Would you like us to come and have Christmas dinner with you tomorrow night? It's a shame you'll have to spend the holiday in here because of your C-section."

I hesitated. The last thing I wanted to do was hurt her feelings, but I preferred to spend the day alone with Mike and Cookie. Our first Christmas as a family. It didn't matter that it would be in a hospital, as long as we were together. "I'll let you know."

Grandma Rosa rose. "Sally and the baby need their rest. We should go. I must get dinner ready for tonight, and there is church as well."

"Don't worry about Spike," Johnny assured us. "I stopped and picked him up last night. We'll keep him at our house for now."

After I had kissed everyone and they'd left the room, my grandmother lingered behind. She smiled at us, her wise eyes thoughtful. "I will make Christmas dinner and bring it tomorrow night. Your *pazza* parents can stay away for one day, *cara mia*. It will not hurt them."

"Does that include a cheesecake?" I asked hopefully.

"But of course." She patted Mike on the cheek and then kissed Cookie's forehead. "I am so happy for you both. She is a true blessing, and what did you say? One tough cookie. Look at all she had to endure to get here."

I pressed my cheek against Cookie's soft face. "Yes, I know. It still scares me when I think about it."

Grandma Rosa pursed her lips. "We never know what tomorrow will bring, my dear. She must always come first."

I gave an involuntary shudder. "Grandma, you're scaring me."

"I do not mean to." She reached for my hand. "I realize that you did everything you could to keep yourself out of danger from that horrible man. He has gone to the hammer and will not bother you again."

"Slammer," I corrected.

"Whatever. I would like to think that all these brushes with death are over for you, but something tells me that is not the case. Your *pazza* father and I do not agree on many things, but he is right. You must be more careful because this little girl needs her mother."

"I promise. She'll always come first, and I'll never put her in danger." Cookie started to fuss, so I began to nurse her, stroking her cheek with my finger. Yes, my baby had gone through a lot to get here. Family had always come first with me, and that would never change. Was it possible to get this murder hex off my head?

Grandma Rosa had once told me that my destiny on this earth was to help people. I would never turn my back on anyone who needed it, but my priorities had changed with the baby's birth. She and Mike were the most important people in my world. I knew how fragile life could be and intended to make every minute of mine count.

Mike kissed the top of my head. "I'm going to walk your grandmother to her car. It's a bit icy out there. Then I'm going to grab something to eat from the cafeteria. Can I get either of my princesses anything?"

I made a face. "You're going to have to change that."

His brow wrinkled. "Change what?"

I shifted the baby in my arms. "You always call me princess. We can't have two princesses."

"No, we can't." He grinned. "I guess you've just been promoted to queen."

CHAPTER TWENTY-ONE

———

The baby didn't nurse long before she fell back asleep. I was about to get out of bed and place her in the bassinet when there was a tap at my door. "Come on in."

Brian strode into the room in full police uniform. He took his hat off and smiled at me. "Wow. Congratulations, Sally. Ally told me that you'd had a girl."

"I haven't even seen Ally." I gestured for him to sit. "News travels fast in this hospital, huh?"

"Yeah, it's gossip central around here." He sat down in the chair and stared at Cookie on my lap. "She's beautiful. You must be so happy."

"I am." I still couldn't believe she was all mine as I stared down into her perfect little face. "I have everything that I've ever wanted now."

Brian was silent, and the moment felt a bit awkward, so I changed the subject. "Did you get a chance to talk to Farley?"

"Yes, I questioned him this morning." Brian ran a hand over the unshaven stubble on his chin. He looked tired. "The guy is seriously missing a few screws. It may have been wrong of Tatiana not to tell him about the abortion, but he still thinks he was justified in killing her. Kind of an eye for an eye from his perspective. He has no regrets about Damian either." His green eyes met mine and were troubled. "It's like the guy doesn't have a soul, Sally. You've encountered quite a few crazies in your life, but Farley is definitely at the top of the list."

I exhaled sharply. "The sooner he goes away, the better for me."

He nodded in agreement. "Don't worry. He won't be bothering you again. It's your misfortune that you were in the wrong place at the wrong time. Those two guys needed a car and saw yours. When Farley found out that you knew Damian, it was the perfect opportunity for him. The ironic part is that, for once in your life, you tried to stay out of trouble, but it found you anyway."

With any luck, it would stay away forever, but I guessed that might not happen, as my grandmother had predicted earlier. "I didn't have a chance to thank you for last night." He'd been the first one to arrive on the scene, or so I'd been told. "I didn't get to thank Nick either. Did you talk to him?"

Brian drew his eyebrows together. "Are you talking about the same guy from your carjacking?"

I shifted in the bed and winced from the pain, careful not to disturb Cookie lying in my lap in a warm little bundle. "Yes. Did you see him?"

He shook his head with regret. "No, Sally, I'm sorry. You were alone when I got to the bakery—well, except for that whack job, of course. He was starting to come around, you were out cold, and it absolutely terrified me." His mouth hardened, and he looked directly into my eyes. "I hate to think what might have happened if I hadn't gotten there so quickly."

I didn't want to think about it either. "Please know how grateful I am to you. But everyone thinks I'm crazy. I know that Nick was there, Brian."

He studied me carefully. "You want to know what I think? This might sound strange, but sometimes I think people are sent to watch over us in difficult situations. When I first started on the force in Boston, I pulled a guy over for speeding. I didn't know that he was also higher than a kite on drugs. When I asked for his license, he reached into the glove compartment and then shot me in the shoulder. While I was lying on the ground helpless, he aimed the gun at me again. I know he would have killed me if he'd had the chance."

"Oh God," I said in horror. "What happened then?"

Brian went on. "At that moment, as he was standing at the front of the vehicle and I was lying to the side, his car moved forward and hit him. He didn't die, but was hurt badly enough that I had the opportunity to crawl to my car and radio for help. Afterward, he swore up and down that he'd put the brake on.

How do you explain that?"

"Honestly, I think there are some things in this life that can't be explained—things that are beyond our control," I said simply. "It wasn't your time to go, so someone was watching over you that night. The way that Nick watched over me."

He nodded. "Exactly. You know what you saw, and that's what matters. Don't worry about what everyone else says. You've got more important things to think about." He smiled down at Cookie, sleeping like an angel. "Like this little lady. By the way, what's her name?"

I beamed. "Her given name is Corinne, but we've decided to call her Cookie for short."

He burst into laughter. "That's perfect. In a few years, you're going to have another helper in your bakery."

"How about you?" I asked slyly. "Any little helpers in your future?"

A shadow passed over his face, and for a moment, I was afraid that my question had offended him.

"I definitely want kids," Brian said after a beat. "And I think I'm ready for them. Ally and I postponed the wedding date a couple of times, as you might have heard. But that was her doing, not mine." He stared at me earnestly, as if he wanted to be sure that I believed him. "I'm ready to make a commitment to her. It's taken me a while to get over—"

I sucked in a breath and prayed he wouldn't finish the sentence. Thankfully, he didn't.

"Anyhow," Brian continued, "we're getting married on Valentine's Day." His face reddened. "It's going to be a small affair, only family."

"There's no need to explain," I said gently. "I'm really happy for you. For both of you." Sure, Brian and I were friends, but I didn't think Ally would want me at her wedding, and I couldn't blame her. They needed to live their own lives, and I intended to do the same.

Brian rose to his feet. "I've got to get back to the station. Are you taking a long maternity leave from the bakery?"

"A few weeks, and then I plan on bringing the baby to work with me." I watched her little chest rise and fall and felt a tightness in my own—love, no doubt. "I don't want to be away from her."

"You're going to make a terrific mother, Sally," Brian said gruffly. He placed a hand on the doorknob and then turned around. "Does this mean that the police department can rest easy now? Are you and Josie hanging up your sleuthing aprons for good?"

I winked. "Don't worry. I'm sure we'll manage to come up with something."

* * *

The clock on the wall was about to strike midnight, but I couldn't sleep. When I was a little girl, I'd always had a difficult time falling asleep on Christmas Eve. Resignedly, I got out of bed, a slow and painful process these days. Slowly I walked to the window and stared out into the deserted parking lot below. The snow had stopped several hours ago. Someone had been in the Christmas spirit and had even made a snowman outside, decorating him with a Santa hat.

The room was quiet and warm. Cookie was in her bassinet, although she'd probably wake up to nurse soon. Mike was lying on his back in the hospital bed, snoring softly. They both looked content and peaceful. Mike had gone home earlier to shower and change. He'd looked tired, but he'd insisted he wanted to spend the night with us. He was going to be such a wonderful father.

The nurse had told me that Santa would be stopping by the maternity ward tomorrow morning and that all the babies were dressed in Christmas stockings for the occasion. I couldn't wait to snap pictures of Cookie in hers.

I turned and picked up the pile of greeting cards Josie had brought with her earlier and began to open them. The news of the baby and my most recent brush with death had spread like wildfire which was typical for the Colwestern grapevine. In fact, good old Jerry Maroon had even mentioned my baby in his column this morning. Was he standing outside the hospital when I delivered Cookie? At least this headline had been somewhat of an improvement. *Former Murder Suspect Delivers Baby after Almost Being Murdered Herself.* Good grief. This was *not* going into Cookie's scrapbook.

Josie and Rob had sent flowers and so had a couple of our regular customers. Mrs. Gavelli had sent a handmade baby blanket over with my grandmother, and to my relief, it was pink, not black.

A few of the cards had rattles attached to the envelopes. One customer had even sent a teddy bear. Some of the envelopes contained gift cards, which was thoughtful but not necessary. I suspected they felt guilty about deserting the bakery during the past week. Oh well. It didn't matter anymore. I was blissfully happy and had no intention of holding any grudges. Life was too short for that.

During Josie's visit, she'd mentioned how several of our regulars had placed large last-minute orders, claiming they'd forgotten to do so earlier. Josie had baked from dawn to dusk, and they'd still run out of Christmas tree and thumbprint jelly cookies. I deemed that a successful day.

I sat down in the chair next to my bed and finished opening the rest of the cards, smiling as I noted the names on each one. I made a mental note to send thank you cards for the gifts when I got home. Filled with happiness, I glanced around the room. My little family was still out like a light. Even though we were in a hospital, it was the best Christmas that I'd ever had.

The last card had no writing on the front. I tore it open and found, to my amusement, that it was a Christmas card instead of a congratulations one. Santa waved at me from a sleigh laden with gifts underneath the caption *Hope This Is Your Best Christmas Yet!*

My Santa phobia had disappeared, and I opened the card with interest. The inside was blank except for five words. Someone had written in block letters with a red felt-tip marker, *Always Believe.*

It was signed, *Your friend, Nick.*

I rose from the chair and stared out the window again, the card clutched tightly between my hands. It was after midnight, and I thought I heard bells in the distance, perhaps from the hospital chapel. Cookie was exactly a day old.

There was a full moon sitting high in the sky, its beam of light shining directly down on me. Despite the cold glass, I was warmed from head to toe. I stared up at the moon for several minutes, thinking about how lucky I was. A shadow passed over the moon, and I blinked. Was that a falling star? Or something else?

I pressed my nose against the glass and continued to watch the moon. The image did not reappear, but that didn't matter. I knew what I'd seen, and the thought made me smile.

"Merry Christmas," I whispered. The light from the moon glowed brighter—a shining, powerful beacon that stood out against the still night. "I'll always believe."

RECIPES

Chocolate-filled Cookie Cups

Ingredients:
1½ cups all-purpose flour
½ teaspoon salt
½ teaspoon baking soda
½ cup (4 ounces) unsalted butter, softened
¾ cup packed brown sugar
1 egg, room temperature
1 teaspoon vanilla extract
1 cup semisweet chocolate chips

Preheat the oven to 350° F. Grease mini muffin pans that have 12 or more cups each or use mini paper baking cups. In a medium bowl, whisk together the flour, salt, and baking soda. In another large mixing bowl, beat the butter and brown sugar until light and creamy, about 2–3 minutes. Beat in the egg and vanilla. Gradually beat in the flour mixture. Stir in the chocolate chips. Roll the dough into 1-inch balls (roughly 1 tablespoon each) and add to each cup in the muffin pan. Bake 10-12 minutes or until cookies fill the cup, are done in the middle, and golden brown. Using a round teaspoon (or something similar), immediately press down into the center of each cookie cup, making an indentation deep enough to fill later. Cool completely before removing from the pans.

For the filling:
1 cup semisweet chocolate chips
¾ cup sweetened condensed milk
½ teaspoon vanilla extract

In a large heatproof bowl over a pan of simmering water (do not let the bowl touch the water), or double boiler, melt together the chocolate chips and sweetened condensed milk. Remove from the heat and stir in the vanilla.

Immediately fill a piping bag, or a sandwich bag with the tip cut off, and fill each cookie cup. The fudge will harden quickly, so reheat the mixture if needed. Let the chocolate harden before serving. Store in an airtight container for up to 1 week. Makes about 30 cups.

Candy Cane Brownies

Ingredients:
1½ cups butter, room temperature
3 cups sugar
5 eggs, room temperature
1 teaspoon salt
1 teaspoon peppermint extract
¾ cup cocoa powder
2¼ cups all-purpose flour

For the Frosting:
½ cup butter, room temperature
4 cups confectioners' sugar
5 tablespoons heavy whipping cream
½ teaspoon peppermint extract
Garnish:
Coarsely broken candy canes

For the brownies: Preheat oven to 350°F. Line a jelly roll pan (15½"x10½"x1") with parchment paper. Spritz the parchment paper with nonstick cooking spray, then spread the batter evenly in the prepared pan. Cream butter and sugar with an electric mixer on medium speed until light and fluffy, about 3 minutes. Beat in the cocoa powder until thoroughly incorporated and no lumps remain. Beat in eggs, one at a time, then add salt and peppermint extract. Mix well. Gradually add in the flour and stir until completely incorporated. Bake for about 30 minutes or until a wooden skewer inserted in the middle comes out clean. Rest pan on a wire rack until completely cool before proceeding with frosting.

For the frosting: Cream the butter, then slowly add the confectioners' sugar and beat until incorporated completely. Add the peppermint extract. Mix in 4 tablespoons heavy whipping cream. Add additional cream, up to 1 tablespoon, until spreadable consistency is reached. Whip for an additional 3 minutes, until frosting is light and fluffy. Frost the brownies, then cut into 2-inch squares. Garnish each square with bits of broken candy canes right before serving. Makes between 20–30, depending how big you cut them. Do not leave out for too long without refrigerating—during a workday or party should be fine, but then refrigerate leftovers immediately afterward.

Gingerbread Cookies

⅓ cup shortening
1 cup brown sugar
1½ cup dark molasses
½ cup + 3 tablespoons cold water
4 cups all-purpose flour
2 cups whole wheat flour
1 teaspoon allspice
1 teaspoon ginger
1 teaspoon clover
1 teaspoon cinnamon
1 teaspoon salt (optional)
2 teaspoons baking soda
1 teaspoon anise extract (optional)
Raisins (optional)

Preheat oven to 350 °F. Mix together shortening, brown sugar, and molasses in a large bowl. Stir in ½ cup cold water, both kinds of flour, allspice, ginger, clover, cinnamon, salt, and baking soda. If necessary, stir in an additional 3 tablespoons of water. Add anise if using. Wrap in plastic and chill in fridge for at least an hour. Roll out onto a floured board to ½-inch thickness. Cut with decorative cookie or gingerbread cutters. Decorate with raisins if desired.

Bake on a greased cookie sheet or parchment paper for 15–18 minutes. Decorate with icing after cooled. Makes between 3–4 dozen 3-inch cookies.

Almond-And-Lemon-Flavored Macaroons

Ingredients:
One can (8 ounces) or 1 roll (7 ounces) almond paste, cut into small pieces.
⅔ cup sugar
2 egg whites (from two large eggs)
1 tablespoon fresh lemon juice
½–¾ cup slivered almonds
Preheat oven to 325° F. Line baking sheet with parchment paper. Beat almond paste, sugar, egg whites, and lemon juice in a medium bowl with mixer on medium speed until smooth. Drop rounded teaspoons 1-inch apart on prepared baking sheet. Sprinkle with almonds to cover. Press nuts gently to adhere. Bake 15–18 minutes, until tops feel firm and dry when lightly pressed. Cool completely on baking sheet on a wire rack. Makes about 12–15 cookies. Store in an airtight container with waxed paper between layers at a cool room temperature for up to one week or freeze for up to three months.

ABOUT THE AUTHOR

USA Today bestselling author Catherine Bruns lives in Upstate New York with a male dominated household that consists of her very patient husband, three sons, and assorted cats and dogs. She has wanted to be a writer since the age of eight when she wrote her own version of Cinderella (fortunately Disney never sued). Catherine holds a B.A. in English and is a member of Mystery Writers of America and Sisters in Crime.

To learn more about Catherine Bruns, visit her online at:
www.catherinebruns.net

Enjoyed this book? Check out the entire
Cookies & Chance Mysteries series!

www.GemmaHallidayPublishing.com

Printed in Great Britain
by Amazon